PRAISE FOR PJ PARRISH

"Tense, thrilling...you're going to bite your nails."   — *Lee Child*

"The kind of book that grabs you and won't let go. I absolutely loved it. nobody is writing better private eye fiction anywhere than PJ Parrish."   — *Steve Hamilton*

"Powerful stuff...the quiet sadness that underpins it all really got to me, the way Ross Macdonald does. Among my favorite Florida crime writers are Charles Willeford, John D. MacDonald and Ed McBain. I'll have to add PJ Parrish." – *Ed Gorman, Mystery Scene.*

"A stunner of a book. Amazingly skilled at creating a sense of place, PJ Parrish stays true to her characters. I can't wait to see Louis's growth as he learns more about the world."
                                                 – *Romantic Times*

"A gripping atmospheric novel that will remind many of Dennis Lehane. the author's ability to raise goose bumps puts her in the front rank of thriller writers."   —*Publishers Weekly*

"A wonderfully tense and atmospheric novel. Keeps the reader guessing until the end."   —*Miami Herald*

"A standout thriller. An atmospheric story set on the grounds of an abandoned insane asylum, a haunting location that contains many dark and barbarous secrets. With fresh characters and plot, a suspense novel of the highest order."
                                           — *Chicago Sun-Times*

"Opens like a hurricane and blows you away through the final page. It's a major league thriller that is hard to stop reading."
                                             — *Robert B. Parker*

PRAISE FOR THE DAMAGE DONE

"The past and the present come into stunning focus in this brilliantly crafted thriller. You'll love every fast-paced minute spent with Michigan cold case detective Louis Kincaid, as he lifts the lid off a series of horrific unsolved murders and finds himself forced to confront their present-day legacies. Relentlessly plotted, yet filled with poignant family emotion, THE DAMAGE DONE will grip you from start to finish."
— *Jeffery Deaver, #1 International bestselling author of THE CUTTING EDGE.*

"Welcome to the Michigan State Police Special Investigations Unit, where cold cases turn red hot and Louis Kincaid finds a disturbing new home for his skills, his compassion, and his relentless obsession with rendering justice. THE DAMAGE DONE is a gritty thriller with a high-octane pace and a beautifully evoked sense of place."
— *C.J. Box, #1 New York Times bestselling author of THE DISAPPEARED.*

"For the last decade and a half, P.J. Parrish has delivered one fine thriller after another featuring the complex and compelling Louis Kincaid. THE DAMAGE DONE is no exception. With a pace that never flags, dialogue that pops like a string of firecrackers, and a cast of characters so intriguing you can't look away, this newest Kincaid novel highlights the mastery of a writing team at the top of their game."
—*William Kent Kruger, New York Times bestselling author of DESOLATION MOUNTAIN.*

Please join PJ Parrish in supporting independent bookstores. Please visit your favorite local bookstore or visit Indiebound.com for a list of bookstores near you.

OUR NOIR

A collection of short stories and a novella

PJ PARRISH

Our Noir Publishing
TRAVERSE CITY, MICHIGAN

Ordering Information:
Quantity sales. Special discounts are available on quantity purchases by corporations, associations, and others. For details, contact the publisher at the website above

Our Noir/ PJ Parrish — 1st ed.
ISBN 978-1-7320867-5-3

Dedicated to our teachers
Miss Gentry and Miss Diane Stribley
who gave us good grades on our first short stories

A short story is like a kiss in the dark from a stranger.

— Stephen King

This story first appeared in the 2006 anthology DEATH DO US PART, edited by Harlan Coben and published by Mystery Writers of America. Our fellow contributors included Lee Child, Laura Lippman and R.L. Stine. You might recognize this old house if you read our 2018 Louis Kincaid thriller THE DAMAGE DONE. We used it as a model for a house Louis recalls living in during his foster-child years in Detroit. The house always had a strange pull on our imaginations.

ONE SHOT

The house was bigger than he remembered it being. Not in size, but in sadness. It wasn't the dust-shrouded windows or the scarred wood floors. It wasn't the missing posts in the staircase out in the hall. It wasn't even all the rectangles on the fade blue wallpaper, imprints from the picture frames that used to hang there.

It was a feeling, something radiating from the old place the moment he stuck the key into the lock and the front door opened with a sigh that came from somewhere deep, deep inside.

He was standing in the living room. It was quiet, the November drizzle a steady *tick-tick-tick* against the windows. He let out a long slow breath that gathered in a vapor cloud in the still air. He wasn't used to the cold anymore. Maybe it was because he had been away from Michigan for so long and had the thin blood

1

of a Floridian now. Maybe it was because he was older and things just bothered him more.

His eyes lingered on the rectangles on the walls. He was remembering how the sunlight used to flood this room at certain times of the year, bleaching out the blue wallpaper. Now the spots stared back at him like so many blank-eyed ghosts, and for the life of him he couldn't remember what had once hung here. All he could recall was that the walls had been covered with pictures, like that store back home in Florida that sold prints of leopards, landscapes and cheesy abstracts.

Leslie had dragged him into the mall store one day to show him a fake oil of a villa in some nondescript country. It was five hundred dollars and she wanted it for the house. He told her he didn't like fake things in the house – plants, paintings, people — and had gone on to Sears to get a replacement for his broken Craftsman saw.

Two days later, Leslie had come home with a different painting by a guy named Thomas Kinkade. It was of a small-town street with all the houses sporting Christmas wreaths and glowing gold from within. It was eleven hundred dollars, but it was real, Leslie assured him. It came with a letter from the artist himself in which he explained his work: "I find that the places where I feel most comfortable share a feeling of neighborhood...where people come together in good fellowship, and, above all, bright lit homes warmed by the light of love..."

"I hate it, Leslie," he told her. "It makes my teeth hurt just to look at it."

"It's just a picture, Stuart. Why are you always so negative?"

He gave up. Leslie hung Home for the Holidays in the family room.

He was still staring at the blank spots on the wallpaper. Why the hell couldn't he remember even one of the pictures that had hung there?

From somewhere outside he could hear the *boom-thucka-boom* of a car's speakers blaring out rap music. He closed his eyes as the sound grew, coming nearer and building to a crescendo, then tapered off. His heart kept time to the dull beat as it died away down the street.

God, how he hated that music. That awful, soul-numbing monotony of it, digging deep into the chest and brain, pouring through the walls as he tried to watch *The McLaughlin Report* every night until finally he had to go up to Ryan's room and pound on the door, demanding he turn it down.

"Why do you listen to that garbage, Ryan?"

"Jesus, Dad, it's just music. Why are you picking on me again?"

The noise was gone. The house was quiet again. He opened his eyes. What was he doing here? What was he looking for in this old wreck of a place?

He turned and walked slowly through the archway, into the empty dining room with its sconces dangling by wires from the walls. He found his way to the kitchen. It was dark in the afternoon dusk. The countertops were the same pale green tiles, the walls the same ivy print wallpaper yellowed with the years and nicotine. The green linoleum squares were curling. He wondered if anyone had even lived in the place recently.

A noise, somewhere deep in the house. A creak of a door. Footsteps on old wood. But he might have imagined it. He pulled in a breath, holding it.

"Mr. Bowen?"

He didn't move.

"Yoo-hoo! Anybody here? Mr. Bowen?"

He exhaled and went back to the living room.

A pudgy woman in a fur coat was standing at the bottom of the stairs. She spun when she saw him emerge from the shadows.

"My goodness, you startled me!" She came forward, hand thrust out. "Jane Talley," she said. "I'm sorry I'm late. Traffic was brutal."

He shook her hand then took a step back to distance himself from her perfume.

"You'd think no one would be on the roads the day before Thanksgiving," she said, taking a red silk scarf off her hair helmet. "Out gathering those last-minute Butterballs, I guess."

"Thank you for coming on such short notice," he said.

"No problem. You found the key okay?"

"Yes, it was in the mailbox where you said it would be."

"Good." She smiled. "Well! If you don't mind, we need to make this quick. I have to pick up my daughter at the airport. She's coming in from Dallas with the kids. You know, the usual big turkey day, eating and drinking too much, telling family war stories and watching the Lions lose."

When he didn't smile she looked away, surveying the living room. She couldn't quite hide her grimace. But the bright smile was back as she turned to him again. "So! Have you looked around?"

"Some."

She pulled leather tote off her shoulder and dug inside. "Here's the sheet," she said, holding out a paper.

He scanned the paper. 989 Strathmoor, Detroit, Wayne County, Michigan. 2/2 with 1 bath upstairs. Built in 1945. Property taxes $2300. Asking price $145,000. There was a black and white photo of the exterior. The brick of the pseudo-Tudor architecture was hidden behind overgrown evergreens and the windows were covered with iron bars.

Another rap music car was rumbling down the street. He could hear it coming, the music a dirge for an old house in a dying neighborhood. He waited until the sound was gone before looking back at the real estate woman.

She was looking at him expectantly, as if she had somewhere to go. Which she did, of course. He shut his eyes tight, a hand coming up to his temple.

"Mr. Bowen?"

Things were forming in his brain. Images. But they weren't in focus. He knew if he tried he might be able to bring them into focus. But he wasn't sure he was ready to face them.

"Mr. Bowen? Are you okay?"

With great effort, he opened his eyes. She seemed relieved.

"How about if we go look upstairs?" she said.

He nodded, pocketing the paper. She led the way, telling him to mind his step because the staircase wasn't in the best of shape but what could you expect since no one had lived in the place for years even though it had been a pretty house in its day before Detroit started going to pot and the mayor who didn't know his butt from a hole in the ground was letting everything go and no matter what anyone said the new casinos down on the river and in Greek Town were not going to bring people back downtown but this was 1998 after all and who didn't want to live out in suburbs where at least you could walk the streets at night and your kids didn't have to go through metal detectors at school...

His head was pounding by the time they reached the top of the stairs.

"My goodness, it's dark up here," she said, flicking a wall switch to no avail.

He went to the nearest bedroom. It was small and had been painted a bright orange with ugly flower decals on the walls. But he could still see the room as it once was. He was letting the memories come now and he could see things and hear the voices.

The small bed with its tan chenille bedspread. The bookcase with its stacks of comic books. And the nubby blue rug with the Clue board spread out on it.

Colonel Mustard in the library with the gun! Ha! I won again!

You cheated, Stu.

Did not!

Yes, you did.

Did not. Let's play again.

No...

Richie, I didn't cheat. Honest. C'mon, let's play again.

No. I'm tired of this game.

He took off his leather gloves and ran his hand lightly over the door frame, his fingers finding the tiny notches that had measured his and Richie's heights.

"This was my room," he said.

The woman stared at him. "Your...?"

"I grew up in this house," he said, turning away from the bedroom. He could hear her heels on the wood floor as she followed him. He glanced in the master bedroom and then the small bathroom.

"Is that why you want to buy this house?" she asked.

He was silent as he turned to her. She had this strange look on her face, and for a moment he was seeing his wife, Leslie, seeing the same look on her face when he first told her he intended to fly to Michigan the day before Thanksgiving so he could go back and see the house.

"Why?" Leslie had asked him.

"I have to," he answered.

"But what about our dinner? What about your family? Dammit, Stuart, I don't understand this. Don't do this to me. It's Thanksgiving, for God's sake. We should be together."

"That's why I have to go," he said.

He started back down the stairs, ignoring the real estate woman's question. He had no intention of buying the house. He just wanted to see it one more time. Maybe if he saw it he could figure out what had happened.

"So, Mr. Bowen," the woman said, coming up next to him in the living room. "What do you do for a living?"

"I teach."

"Really? How nice. What do you teach?"

"Literature."

He moved away, heading toward the kitchen again so she wouldn't ask him anything else. He didn't want to have to explain that he didn't teach "literature." He was a professor of classics at University of Miami. He taught courses with names like "Ancient Moral Thought and Education." He had full tenure, a house in the Grove, a wife who did volunteer work, a son who didn't do drugs. He had a new Volvo, an aging dachshund, and an unfinished novel in his drawer. He had — he would on occasion admit this, but only to himself — a drinking problem.

He was, to everyone who knew him, a success. He knew, in the deepest corners of his heart, that he was failure. Somewhere along the way, his life had gone off course and he had been stalled — he, Leslie and Ryan. No, not stalled. Wrecked. His life had become derailed and now there they all were, sprawled in their pain, disconnected and bloodied, pretending they didn't hear each other's cries.

It was all his fault. He knew he had to make it right somehow. That is why he had come back here. He knew that suddenly. He had come back here, to this house, to try and save himself and his family. To give it one last shot.

He turned and saw the door.

The real estate woman was at his side. "That just leads to the basement," she said.

"I need to see it," he said.

The woman glanced at her watch and let out a silent sigh that spiraled up in the cold air. He could see in her eyes what was in her head: that he was not a potential buyer but just a weird old man on a nostalgia trip.

"Ah, if you don't mind, Mr. Bowen, it's really getting late, and the airport — "

"I need to see the basement," he said.

She hesitated then shrugged. "Suit yourself." Now that she knew any hope of a sale was gone, so was her charm. "You don't mind if I wait here, do you?"

The door stuck when he tried to open it, then gave way with a creak. He stood at the top of the stairs, peering down into the darkness. Cold air wafted up, carrying a smell of dampness and decay.

He started down.

It wasn't until he got to the bottom of the stairs that he realized he was holding his breath. He let it out now, slowly, as he looked around. His heart grew smaller in his chest. They had let it go, whoever had lived here after him. They had let the mildew grow, let the dirt and years take over. He could see it, even though the light coming through the small casement windows was thin. He could see that it was all in ruins.

The bar was still there, the one his father had built, but it was heaped with sagging boxes. The knotty pine paneling was still on the walls but it was dark with grime. The shelves were still here, the ones that used to hold boxes of Christmas decorations and his mother's jams, but they were broken and dusted with rat droppings.

He could hear the steady *splat-splat* of water somewhere. He could hear voices, like some forgotten broken song.

Stu? Stu, are you down there?

Yeah, Ma!

Get up here. I gotta get to the A&P before it closes.

Ah, Ma, I don't wanna go. I wanna stay down here with Richie.

I told you, no staying in the house alone.

Ma, I can stay! I'm almost thirteen. C'mon, Ma! We're doing important stuff!

Stu –

We won't leave the basement, Ma. I promise.

Well...okay. I'll be back in an hour and as soon as your father comes home we're going to eat.

Can Richie stay for dinner?

No, not again. Richie needs to go home. I think his mother would like him to come home for a change.

But Ma —

You heard me, Stuart. Not tonight.

There had been an old sofa in the middle of the basement. He could see it clearly, a lumpy thing with itchy red upholstery and cushions that he and Richie used as building blocks for their forts. There had been a card table where his father played poker with his friends and where he and Richie laid out their papers and crayons, where they conspired, head to head, making their own comic books. They called their super-hero Brain Boy, and he had the power to kill someone just by thinking about it. He had made up the stories and Richie had drawn the pictures – beautiful pictures! They were going to publish their own comics when they grew up. They would do it together, just like they had always done things.

That was the plan. Grow up and get famous and show everyone. Show Richie's father that drawing wasn't a "homo thing."
Show Nate Carson and those dumb boys at school, make them
all sorry for what they had done, all the mean things they had
said. Grow up and get famous. Grow up and forget about that
time Nate had pushed Richie to the asphalt, calling him a dumb
Polack, busting his glasses and bloodying his nose. Grow up and
forget about those girls watching and laughing. Grow up and forget about telling and then finding his cat handing dead from a
stop sign two nights later. Grow up and make them all sorry.
That was their plan, Stuart Bowen and Richie Koweski, comic
book heroes.

He looked toward the farthest, darkest corner of the basement. He could just make out the door that he knew led to the
small room. He closed his eyes and the images went away. But
the voices didn't.

Richie, what's the matter with you today?

Nothing.

You wanna walk down to the party store. I got a quarter. We —

Nah...

You sick, Richie?

No.

Then what's the matter?

I told you, nothing!

How come you weren't at school today?

I dunno.

Okay...what you wanna do then?

I dunno.

We could go watch Mr. Wizard.

Uh-uh.

You wanna work on Brain Boy?

Nah.

Cripe, Richie, if you don't wanna do anything, maybe you should go home.

I don't want to go home. My dad is home.

So?

He's drinking beer.

Big deal. My dad drinks beer.

Your dad doesn't hit you. I don't want to go home, Stu.

Yeah, well, if you're gonna be a puke, then maybe you should!

Silence. He could still hear the silence. The terrible silence that had filled with basement as Richie just sat there, slumped on the red sofa. He could still remember what he had thought at that moment, that Richie looked like one of those rubber punching bags, those things with the clown faces, a punching bag that had a leak and was all deflated.

His eyes went again to the door in the corner. He knew he had to go over there and open it but he couldn't move. He was shivering, and when he wiped his nose, his hand was shaking. He had come thousands of miles. He had waited forty years. Just to see what was in that room. If he didn't go in, if he backed out now, there would be no chance. No chance for him and Leslie and Ryan. No chance at all.

His feet moved, carrying him to the door, as if he were being propelled by some outside force. When he reached out to the door, he looked down at his hand, at the blue veins standing out in high relief against his chapped white skin, and he had the odd sensation that if was someone else's hand. The metal knob was icy. The door swung inward with a small groan.

The smell of something rotten filled with nostrils. Gray afternoon light filtered in through a broken window, illuminating the tiny room. Sagging shelves holding old baby food jars filled with rusted nails. A wooden work bench dark with mold. Puddles of fetid water on the concrete floor. A decomposing rat. The smell – it was just a brew of all the smells, he knew that.

But there was another smell underneath it, an odd smell, like something metallic. A smell that he had never, ever been able to erase. A smell that had clung to him for decades. A smell that was now pushing its way up over the decay, bringing everything back up with it.

He couldn't stop it. It was all coming out now, and he couldn't stop it.

The metallic smell was everywhere. The blood was everywhere. Richie was lying on the concrete floor.

Richie? Richie? Richie!

Silence. And that metallic smell hanging in the air.

Oh, God, Richie!

Blood. Richie's blood. It was everywhere, splattered on the Chessie train calendar on the wall. And bits of Richie's brains. He saw that, too, clinging to the baby food jars and the tools.

He saw the gun in his own hand.

Ma! Ma! Oh, no...Richie! Ma! Come down here, Ma!

But no one came. Finally, he heard a car door slam, heard his mother's footsteps and the sound of her putting away the groceries in the kitchen, heard her call his name. But he couldn't answer. Even when he heard her coming down the stairs, he couldn't answer. He just stayed there, crouched in the corner, holding the gun in his lap as she screamed and screamed.

The house filled up with strangers. A big man in blue took the gun away and led him upstairs to the kitchen. Another man in blue washed the blood from him. Someone made him put on clean clothes, and then they sat him on a chair in the living room and told him not to move. He heard his mother crying in the kitchen.

He just sat there, not moving, listening to it all, feeling his body turn to stone. The only things that moved where his eyes. His eyes moved over all the pictures on the blue-papered walls, jumping from one to another because he knew that as long as he kept looking at those pictures he wouldn't see Richie's shattered head. Finally, when his eyes got tired, he let them rest on one picture – the one over the TV of Jesus touching His glowing heart. He stared at Jesus and Jesus stared back.

Then, suddenly, someone was there, kneeling in front of him. His face was white and his eyes were tear-filled. His father? What was his father doing home? How did he get home so fast?

Stuart...we need to talk.

I didn't mean it. I just got mad. We weren't really fighting.

I know.

It's just...it's just...sometimes Richie —

Stuart, listen to me.

I didn't think he remembered where it was. We only looked at it once. Honest.

What?

Your gun. We didn't really play with it. I just took it out and showed it to Richie. I didn't think he remembered where it was!

His father looked back over his shoulder. There were other people in the living room now, but he hadn't even seen them coming in. Four policemen in blue. A man in a brown suit writing on a pad. The old bald priest from St. Jerome's who smelled of Sen-Sen. And other faces, all just a blur.

His father took him by the shoulders.

Stuey, listen to me...

I didn't mean to —

I know.

I think he was sick, Dad. He didn't go to school today and —

Stuey, be quiet.

I don't know...I don't know what happened.

He felt his father's hands tighten on his shoulders. Felt the warmth of his breath close to his face.

It was an accident, Stuey Boy.

What?

You were playing with the gun. You were showing Richie the gun and it went off. It was an accident.

But Richie —

Stuey Boy. Listen to me. That is what happened. It was just an accident. But everything will be all right.

His father's eyes were steady on him, unblinking. But suddenly, he couldn't look at him. So he looked over his father's shoulder, over to the priest and the police standing together in the corner. His eyes finally found the picture of Jesus on the wall. He focused on it until it went blurry.

Everything after that was blurry, too. The only thing he could remember clearly was packing up his comic books when his family moved away a year later. He found one of Richie's Brain Boy drawings and stuck it inside a Superman so he wouldn't ever lose it. It was years later, after he had come home from college one Christmas that he found out his mother had long ago thrown all the old comics out in the trash.

"Mr. Bowen?"

He opened his eyes and the workroom came into slow focus.

"Yoo-hoo! Mr. Bowen, are you still down there?"

"Yes..." He cleared his throat. "Yes!"

"I really must get going."

"I want to stay. I'll lock up."

"Mr. Bowen, I don't think —"

"I'll leave the key in the box. Please. Please, just go."

A long pause. "All right. Have a happy Thanksgiving, Mr. Bowen."

He looked up, his eyes following the sound of her footsteps to the front of the house. The thud of the door closing and then it was quiet, except for the *splat-splat* of water. The workroom felt as dark and close as the confessional at St. Jerome's.

Forgive me, Father, for I have sinned.

Forgive me, Father, I took your gun out of your toolbox.

Forgive me, Mother, I made you cry and you never stopped.

Forgive me, Father, for I have sinned. I shot Richie.

His mother had taken him to church a week after Richie's funeral. He could still see the priest's bald head, glowing white through the screen of the confessional, could hear his whispered words: God loves the sinners among us most, my son. It was an accident, but everything will be all right. God loves you. For your penance do...

...do forty years. Forty years of waking up sweating at night, forty years of jumping at the sound of cars backfiring, forty years of looking away whenever you saw a blond boy wearing black glasses, forty years of closing down your heart because if you let someone in and they died, it hurt too much.

It was cold in the basement, and he was shivering. He took one last look around the workroom. There was nothing for him here, no absolution, no salvation. There were no answers to the question of what had happened. He backed out of the room and closed the door.

Upstairs, he paused in the living room. It was getting late, the shadows growing into the gloom of the coming winter. He dug in his pocket for his gloves but when he pulled them out, one was missing. He checked his other pockets, scanned the floor, backtracked to the kitchen, but didn't find it. Ryan had given him the gloves for his birthday and he didn't want to leave with it. But he didn't want to go back in the basement either.

Then he remembered he had taken the gloves off upstairs. Going back up, he spotted the glove on the floor outside the bedroom. As he bent to pick it up, something in his memory shifted. He straightened slowly.

He stared into the bedroom. Suddenly, it was as if someone had switched on a lamp, lighting the dark corners. Suddenly, he could see himself. He was twelve again, sprawled on his stomach on the chenille spread, comic books scattered around him. Then he heard it, heard it clearly, like he had heard it forty years ago. He heard the sharp *pop!* that came from somewhere outside. And he remembered what he had thought in that moment – where did someone get firecrackers in November?

The memories were coming fast now.

What was it that made him realize the sound hadn't come from outside? What was it that made him go downstairs, through the kitchen, and back down to the basement? What was it that made him open the door to his father's workroom?

He couldn't remember. But what he did remember was...

Oh, God.

Richie lying there on the concrete floor, the gun inches from his palm.

He could remember screaming. *Richie! Richie! What did you do?*

It was all there in his head now, playing like a tape he had thought was long erased. He could remember calling Richie a puke and telling him to go home. He could remember going upstairs to his room and leaving Richie alone in the basement.

Then...then...

In the basement again, where he picked up the gun because he thought Richie might still be alive and he wanted to get the gun away from him. He could remember staring at Richie's oozing wound and throwing up. He could remember sitting on the cold concrete floor because he didn't want Richie to be alone. He could remember watching the blood crawl across the gray floor to the drain.

Then...then...

Upstairs in the living room now, watching the gurney with the small lump under the blue covering being wheeled out the front door. The outline of his father's gun in the plastic bag as the policeman carried it away. His mother's sobs in the kitchen and the priest's calm voice. He could hear the priest talking to Richie's father. He could see them all gathered in a knot, looking at him and whispering.

Then...then...

His father's face before him. He could feel the pressure of his hands on his shoulders and hear his words again: You were playing with the gun. You were showing Richie the gun and it went off. It was just an accident. But everything will be all right.

"No."

The sound of his own voice startled him. The empty bedroom came back into focus.

They knew. They all knew.

His mother, Richie's parents, the police, the priest, and his own father. They all knew Richie had shot himself. They all knew what had really happened, and they let him believe that they didn't.

He couldn't breathe. And his heart felt like a dying animal in his chest, heavy with pain, struggling to keep going. He had to get out of the house.

He stumbled up the stairs and through the living room. Outside, he stopped on the sidewalk and bent over, feeling sick. He pulled a deep breath of cold air into his lungs, then another. Finally, when he felt steadier, he straightened. He looked back at the house.

The sting of tears came to his eyes, and he wiped a shaking hand over his face. Then, slowly, he walked to his rental car parked at the curb. He got in but just sat there, staring straight ahead. The sleet had caused the windshield to freeze over, giving the black bare trees a wavy, surreal look. He sat perfectly still, hands on the wheel, his breath pluming in the cold womb of the car.

Why? Why had they done it, this conspiracy of parents, priests and police? All the people who were supposed to protect him had betrayed him. And his own father had knelt before him and lied, told him it was an accident, let him take the blame, and told him everything would be all right.

But it wasn't an accident and everything wasn't all right.

The tears fell silently down his face. Slowly, he reached over and popped open the glove compartment. The gun was ice cold in his hand as he pulled it out. He stared at it, feeling its weight in his hand, thinking how light it felt compared to then.

No one knew he had it. After his father died in 1972, he had come home to help his mother and he found the gun in a box in the closet. It had been cleaned and oiled and had one bullet in its chamber. He took it back to college, wrapped in an old sweater, and stuck it in a footlocker. The locker was with him when he took the job in Florida and when he and Leslie moved into the house in the Grove. When Ryan was born, he took the gun out to the garage and locked it in a toolbox. For the last seventeen years, it had stayed here. Until last night, when he took it out and carefully packed it in his suitcase for the trip back to Michigan.

His fingers closed around the revolver's grip. He didn't have to look. He knew the bullet was still in there.

The sleet was a steady *tick-tick* on the windshield. His hand was trembling and the revolver was heavy, too heavy to hold any longer. He let it fall to his lap and leaned his cheek against the cold glass of the window.

How long did he stay like that? Minutes, an hour? When he finally opened his eyes, he saw a face. He had to squint to see it, but there was someone watching him from a front window of the nearest house. The face was hardly more than a white blur through the icy windshield, but he could tell the person was watching him.

It took a couple more seconds before the memory registered: Richie's house...that was Riche's old house. He quickly rolled down the window to get a better look, but the face had disappeared.

Rolling the window up, he jumped from the car and started across the street. He realized he was still holding the gun and he quickly slipped it into the pocket of his overcoat. As he approached the porch, a quick memory flashed through his head — Mr. Koweski, out mowing his lawn. It had been the prettiest lawn on the block. But now there was nothing but mud and dead weeds fronting a run-down house with bars on the windows and plastic trash bags on the porch.

He rang the bell. There was a dirty blue plastic bin near the door filled with empty booze bottles. He rang the bell again then opened the sagging screen door and knocked.

After a long time, the door opened just enough for a man to peer out.

"Yeah?"

At first, he didn't recognize him. He had been half-expecting the see the big man with the barrel chest and slicked-back black hair, the man he remembered as Richie's father. But this was just an old man, with ashen skin and dirty gray hair. But the eyes...he remembered those piercing black eyes.

"Mr. Koweski?"

"I ain't buying anything."

"I'm not sell – Mr. Koweski, it's me, Stuart. Stuart Bowen."

"What?"

"Stuart Bowen...I used to live –" He pointed across the street.

The old man's eyes narrowed. "Bowen...Bowen." His eyes shot open. "Stuey? That you, Stuey Boy?"

He cringed at the sound of his old nickname, the one that Mr. Koweski had given him, the one he hated so much because it made him feel so little.

"Yes, yes, it's me. Stuey Boy."

The old man's mouth was hanging open and for a moment, he looked like he might fall over. But his hand gripping the door was like a claw. He pushed the door open wide.

"Come in, then," he said. "I'm not heating the outdoors here."

Inside, he followed the old man through the dim living room toward the lighted kitchen beyond. Dark outlines of old sagging furniture, piles of yellowed newspapers, overflowing ashtrays. The gloom was undercut with a foul smell, something musty and unclean, as if the place hadn't been opened up to sunlight or other human beings in a long time. He remembered suddenly that about four years after his own family had moved away, his father had seen Mrs. Koweski's funeral announcement in the *Free Press*. Heart failure, his father read. Broken heart, his mother had responded.

In the kitchen, the old man moved to the stove, picked up a kettle then let it fall back to the grimy burner. "I'm out of coffee. You want a drink instead?"

"No, thank you."

The old man waved to the table. "Have a seat."

He slipped into one of chairs of the yellow Formica dinette set. He had a vague memory of eating baloney sandwiches with

Richie at the same table, with Mrs. Koweski hovering nearby, wan and wary-eyed.

The old man came to sit in a chair opposite. He was holding a tumbler of clear liquid and pulled the lapels of his stained bathrobe over his chest.

"Stuey Boy," he said softly, shaking his head.

He didn't respond.

"I heard you moved to Florida," the old man said.

"Yes. A long time ago."

The old man took a drink, running a hand over his unshaven face. "Life been good to you?"

When there was no answer, the old man took another drink. The smell of gin was overpowering.

"Mr. Koweski –"

"Well, you didn't ask, but things aren't so hot for me. You can see that for yourself. Neighborhood's gone to hell and I waited too damn long to sell. The wife wouldn't have it...said she wanted to stay here no matter what. Then she died and here I am."

The kitchen was quiet.

"What the hell you doing back here, anyway?" the old man asked.

"What?"

"Why'd you come back?"

"Richie. I came back because of Richie."

The old man stared hard at him. He didn't move, not a muscle, not an eyelash. But something in his eyes seemed to draw inward, as if he was waiting for something he knew was coming, like a punch-drunk fighter waiting for the last blow.

"It was an accident. That day in the basement. I didn't do it."

The black eyes were still waiting.

"Richie killed himself, Mr. Koweski."

Still, the old man didn't move. Then, slowly, he brought the tumbler up to his lips. His hand was shaking. He finished off the gin and set the glass down on the table, wiping a hand across his mouth. He rose, leaning heavily against the table, and took the empty glass to the counter. He stood at the sink, his back turned, his head down.

"Mr. Koweski?"

No response.

"I know what happened. Did you hear me? I know that Richie killed himself."

The old man spun around. "Shut up! Don't talk about that!"

For a second, he was stunned into silence. When he finally spoke, it was a struggle to keep his voice calm. "I need to talk about it, Mr. Koweski, and you're the only one left to hear me."

The black eyes bored into him. "No! I won't talk about it. I don't want to talk about things like that. Not in my house! This is a good Catholic house, and it's a sin. What you're saying about Richie is a sin!"

The word, spat out in a hiss, hung in the cold air of the kitchen, and he could only stare at the old man. Sin? Is that what this was all about? Is that why they had done it? Richie's parents, the priest, his own father – is this why they had let him carry the blame, so the stain of suicide could be wiped clean?

He brought up his hands and covered his face. The only sound was the hum of the refrigerator.

"Stuey?"

The old man's voice was a pleading whisper, but he didn't want to look at him.

"Stuey Boy?"

When he took his hands from his face he was astonished to see tears in the old man's eyes.

"It was just an accident. Can't you see that, Stuey Boy?"

He watched the tears fall down the old man's cheeks. And, slowly, something changed, like the last piece of a jigsaw puzzle slipping into place.

Tears in black eyes. Hands on his shoulders. And that smell...the smell of someone's breath so close, with its stink of beer.

Stuey Boy. Nobody else had ever called him that. It hadn't been his father who had knelt before him that day. It hadn't been his father who had set the whole thing in motion, made him distrust the truth, all the people he loved and believed in, and himself. In his confused and frightened mind, it had all been one huge blur, and he realized now that his father hadn't even been there. It had been Richie's father. He had been the one in the house that day who started the long lie.

Just an accident, Stuey Boy.

He reached into the pocket of his overcoat and pulled out the revolver. The old man's eyes widened when he saw it.

"It was you."

The old man drew back against the counter. "What?"

"I know what you did to me, Mr. Koweski."

The old man's eyes were locked on the revolver.

"But it's over now."

The old man's eyes shot up. They were watery and wide with fear. But he could see other things in those black eyes now – shame, guilt, loneliness, and fatigue, a fatigue that he could see was as long and heavy and aching as his own.

Stuart Bowen stood up. "I don't need this anymore."

He set the gun on the Formica table.

"Goodbye, Mr. Koweski."

He turned and left the kitchen. He didn't stop as he retraced his steps through the dark house and out into the cold

November evening. It was only when he was in the car that he allowed himself to pull in a long slow breath.

He could feel his heart beating in his chest, feel the quiet steady thud of his life. He started the engine and turned on the heater. For a moment, he just sat there, waiting for the car to warm up as he stared at his old house.

He closed his eyes and exhaled.

The sharp *pop!* made him start. He opened his eyes and looked up at Richie's house. There was no face at the window.

For a moment – just a moment – he thought of going back in. But then he put the car in drive and moved forward, without looking back.

Pride was written for DETROIT NOIR, an
anthology published in 2007 by the
distinguished Akashic Books, edited by
E.J. Olsen and John C Hocking. The Noir series
feature themed stories all set in specific
locations around the world. We were
honored to be among the
contributors who included
Loren Estleman, Megan Abbott
and Joyce Carol Oates. The germ of this story came from Kris,
who lived in a tiny apartment in Royal Oak, Michigan, near the
Detroit Zoo. And yes, when the wind was right, she could hear
the lions roaring at night.

PRIDE

*T*onight, I have the windows open to catch what little breeze
there is, and as I lay in my damp sheets, my face turned toward the gauzy glow of the streetlight outside, I can hear
them. The lions are roaring.

*It starts low, a moaning prelude. Then it builds, drifting to me in
my bed with the shifts of the heavy August air, until it becomes a
distant but full-throated roar.*

Aaaa-OUUU. Aaaa-OUUUUUUU.

*I listen, my body tense, until it finally dies into a series of stac-
cato grunts.*

Huh, huh, huh.

*I am two miles away from the lions, safe in my basement studio
apartment just a block off Woodward Avenue. I know the lions are*

secured behind a moat. *They are fed twice a day, cosseted by their caretakers at the Detroit Zoo. They want for nothing.*

So why do they roar at night?

It starts again.

Aaaa-OUUU. Aaaa-OUUUUU.

I look toward the corner where the yellow-white beam from the streetlight falls across the bureau and brings the steel of my gun to life.

I press my palms over my ears and close my eyes.

Baker was waiting at my desk when I got to work the next morning. He had made my coffee for me.

"You look like hell," he said, holding out my chipped white mug. The rim still had yesterday's lipstick on it but I didn't care.

"I couldn't sleep," I said.

"You need to do something about that," he said.

I nodded as I sipped the coffee. He had even remembered the Splenda. After four years of riding together, it made me feel good that he remembered how I took my coffee. My ex had never seemed to get that one down.

"Drink up, we have a call," Baker said.

I looked at him over the rim of the mug. "How bad?"

He held my eye for moment but didn't say anything before he turned away to pick his jacket off the chair. That explained the waiting coffee. It was going to be a really bad one.

We drove through a sticky morning rain, moving away from the Central District station house on Woodward. For once, I hadn't put up a fight when Baker told me he was going to drive. I just sat back in the seat, watching the slow sweep of the windshield wipers.

Baker took a right into Brush Park. A century ago, the neighborhood had been home to the city's elite. But now it was block after block of decaying Victorians, weedy empty lots, and the collapsing brick caverns of abandoned boarding houses. We called it The Zone, the nickname coming from the government E-Zone program that was funneling millions of dollars into Detroit's decaying core.

The E stood for Empowerment, the politicians said, and there were signs of life here and there – a new Blimpie's over on Mack, an old factory being converted to lofts, a few rehabbed mansions reclaimed from ruin. And at night, when the Tigers had a home game, the southern horizon burned bright with the lights from Comerica Park. But for most people here, the empowerment hadn't trickled down enough to ease the pain of their daily lives. To most people in The Zone, E still meant empty.

Literally empty, I thought, as I stared out the window.

Over the past couple decades, in the name of renewal, whole blocks of blighted and burned-out houses had been demolished, leaving vast stretches of weeds and grass. Untrimmed trees formed tunnels over the pocked streets. Wild pheasants had taken to roosting in the rafters of the rotting houses. The Zone had the aching loneliness of an abandoned prairie town.

As we turned onto John R, I found myself looking for the small reminders of the lush life that had once thrived here. A set of stairs leading up to nowhere, the ornate carvings still visible in the crumbling concrete. A listing red brick chimney covered with the creeping pink blossoms of wild sweet pea vines. A rusted stop sign standing sentry on a corner where no one came anymore.

But then, the surprise of a lone house, bars on the windows and plastic flowers in the yard. And another, its sagging porch strung with Christmas lights. People hanging on, barricading themselves in their homes against the drug dealers and prostitutes, waiting for the city fathers to figure it all out.

I stole a glance at Baker's Sharpei profile, with the ever-present mint-flavored toothpick hanging from his lip. None of this ever seemed to bother him. He was driving slowly, like he always did, a sharp contrast to my own gas-brake-gas-brake style. Baker kept an even flow on most everything. Even on calls like this, even when he knew what we were going to see.

"How old?" I asked.

"Four months," he said.

The rain had stopped by the time we pulled up to the house. There was a small crowd gathered by the steps, women mostly, their arms crossed over their chests or clutching kids to their thighs. The low tire-whir of the nearby Fisher Freeway filled my ears.

Baker turned to me. "You ready?"

Usually someone – often the mother but on rare occasions the male in the house — takes the child to the emergency room. Driven by a fleeting clarity of what they have done, they hope that the limp body in their arms can be miraculously transformed back into a baby.

That was not what had happened in the house on John R.

When the responding officers arrived, the child was still in its bed. By the time I entered the blue bedroom, the eyes of three stuffed animals – a bear, a rabbit and a zebra – looked down upon an empty crib. With its broken slats, it looked like a wooden cage.

Baker nudged me, indicating I should step aside to let the photographer do his job. The camera flash brightened the blood on the tangled yellow blanket. The air smelled of sour diapers.

I heard a woman crying. Between her sobs, she whispered the name Tommy. I followed the sound back to the living room, pulling my notebook from my jacket.

The woman sat on a green sofa. When her eyes came up, she focused first on Baker, then on me, making that female-to-female connection. I knew from experience she had some vague hope that I was the one person in this group of stone-faced strangers who might understand why her baby had died at the hands of her man. I resented it and I wanted to slap her. Instead, I sat down next to her.

"What was your son's name?" I asked.

"Justin."

"And your boyfriend's name?"

"Tommy Freeman." It was his name she had called out, not her baby's.

"Do you know here he is right now?" I asked.

"Probably at his brother's."

I took down all the information in my notebook. I wrote slowly, postponing the final part of my interview, the part that in all my years as a cop had never gotten any easier. I learned a long time ago that these women often changed their stories when they realized their boyfriends or husbands were going to prison. Sometimes, they recanted everything. Sometimes, they took full blame themselves.

I set a small tape recorder on the scarred coffee table near the woman's knees.

"Can you tell me what happened?"

"The baby stressed Tommy out. He works nights, and the constant crying..."

I nodded, my eyes closing over a burn of tears. I knew I wouldn't cry. I had this way of absorbing tears back inside my head. Baker once told me that if I didn't let them out once in a while, they'd back up in my brain and began to ferment. He had meant it as a joke, but I didn't laugh.

"Please don't hurt him when you pick him up," the woman whispered.

I said nothing and stood up. The creamy scent of formula was in my nose and I looked around. A blue plastic baby bottle sat on the end table.

"You'll need to go with the officers down to the station, ma'am," I said.

She looked at me in confusion. "But I didn't do anything."

"I know," I said.

Baker stopped at the traffic light. The heat rose in wavering vapors from the hot asphalt, dissipating into the pale yellow sky. There was a Sulphur smell in the air that pricked my nostrils even through the closed car windows.

"Can we stop at Angela's?" I asked.

He nodded and turned right, heading to an apartment building over on Winder. I had meet Angela about three years ago. She was working in a strip club up on Eight Mile, trying to do the best she could for her twelve-year-old daughter. Angela had just married Curtis Streeter, a mostly unemployed construction worker with flat black eyes and the names of his two ex-wives tattooed on his bicep. As a wedding gift, he had added Angela's name to his arm.

It was two nights after the wedding that Baker and I made our first visit to their place. We found Angela crumbled in the corner of the tiny kitchen, bloody hand prints smeared on the oven door. The daughter was in her bed with a split lip and her hair chopped off above her ears with dull scissors. Punishment by her stepfather for sassing back.

Angela had been strong at first, fueled by her pain and the sight of her daughter's ragged hair. But in the days after, she began to withdraw, the pain turning to regret and self-blame, and I knew that without Angela's testimony, Streeter would walk free.

For the first time in my career, I went the extra mile for a victim. I spent nights digging into Streeter's past, but I didn't find anything that could send him away. But I did find a few things that I hoped might steel Angela's resolve.

A few years before he hooked up with Angela, Streeter had been living with a woman who had an infant son. Six weeks into their relationship, the mother carried her dead son into an emergency room. The baby had died of a head injury, like his brain had ricocheted around inside his skull, the doctors said. The mother said that the baby had fallen down some stairs. No one believed her. But when Streeter's alibi was backed up by three of his punk friends, the only thing the cops could do was charge the mother with neglect.

I pulled out the coroner's photos of the dead child and I showed them to Angela, telling her Streeter had shaken that baby to death. A week later, Angela stood in court and begged the judge to put Streeter away. Because Streeter had a record and his battery charge on Angela violated his probation, an impatient judge had given him seven years.

In the four years I had been working the special crimes unit, I could count on one hand the number of abuse cases that came close to a successful resolution. Angela's was one of them, and I had been keeping tabs on her ever since. Maybe I took a sort of pride in the fact that I had helped her turn some corner.

That's why I had asked Baker to swing by. That, and I needed something to wipe the image of Justin's bloody crib from my head.

*　　　*　　　*

The outside of Angela's building was as bad as I remembered. But behind the triple deadbolts she had fixed up her place. Fresh mauve paint, rose-patterned curtains I knew she had made herself. The place smelled of simmering beef and green beans.

Baker posted himself at the window to watch our cruiser below. Last week on this same street a squad car had been stripped while an officer was inside taking a report.

Angela emerged from the kitchen carrying a can of Vernor's ginger ale. She looked good, even with a few extra pounds. Her hair was bright yellow from a recent coloring. Men tipped well, for blond hair, she had once told me.

When she handed me the can of pop, an odd scent drifted off her body. Someone who had given birth would have recognized it more quickly, but it wasn't until I picked up on Angela's expression – child-bright with a secret – that it hit me. The smell was breast milk.

"I had a baby," she said.

I scanned the room for evidence that a man now lived here. I saw nothing except a baby seat pushed into the corner near the television.

"When?"

"Three months ago. Want to see him?"

I followed her back to the bedrooms. The first room was painted pink, adorned with posters of pop stars and kittens. The daughter's room. She'd be fifteen or so now.

At the door of Angela's room, I slowed, but she waved me over to the bassinet by the bed.

A halo of curls around a chubby face. Long brown lashes that fluttered with dreams. His tiny body filled only a third of the mattress.

"Who's the father?" I asked.

Angela picked up the baby and placed a soft kiss on his head. "He's out of the picture," she said. "He was married, and I'm okay with that. He paid for everything, though. Still sends me money when he can."

I found the news oddly comforting. "So you're doing okay?"

Angela nodded yet wouldn't meet my eyes. There was something she wasn't telling me, but I wasn't sure I should push. Baker had said I couldn't be protector and friend to the victims I met. The line between them was too thin.

"Sheffield," Baker called out.

Something in the way he said my name compelled me quickly back to the living room. I stopped short, staring into a pair of flat black eyes.

Curtis Streeter stood there, smiling at me.

I didn't smile back.

"Curtis has been paroled."

Angela's voice was small behind me. I didn't turn to look at her, just kept my eyes on Streeter.

Angela sidled past me, still carrying the baby and going to Streeter's side. He gave her an odd hug, his hand gently pushing the baby to Angela's hip so he could flatten himself against her body. When he broke the embrace, his eyes came back to my face. He wasn't smiling anymore. It was clear he remembered me.

"He doesn't have any place to go," Angela said. "I'm letting him move back in."

My eyes flicked to Baker, still standing by the window. He wasn't watching Streeter. He was watching me. He gave me a subtle shake of his head. I turned away.

Tonight, I have the windows closed, even though it is still eighty degrees. I lay here in my narrow bed, staring at the shadows. Finally, I can't stand it any longer and go to the window, throwing it open. The heavy night air pours over me.

I stand at the small casement window, looking up at the ground that encloses me, and then up further to the small slice of night sky I can glimpse. No stars, no moon.

I crawl back to my bed, my head thick with sleeplessness. Just as I dare to close my eyes, it starts, a single low roar.

Then another in answer, and finally, a third, forming a raw chorus of overlapping, repetitive bellows.

Closer, a night bird calls, its tiny sharp pleading punctuated by the roaring.

The night has awakened, and its creatures – large and small – are proclaiming themselves to the world.

"What's with you today?"

I stayed silent. A part of me was glad that Baker picked up on my mood because I hadn't been able to think of a way to tell him what I needed to.

"Sheffield, what the hell is wrong?"

I let out a long breath. "I'm thinking of bagging it."

"Bagging what?"

"This. I can't do it anymore. I can't take it anymore."

Baker was quiet, chewing on his toothpick, his hands steady on the wheel. The soft chatter of the radio filled with car.

"This got anything to do with Angela?" he asked.

"No. Maybe. Shit, I don't know."

"Sheffield, for crissake..."

I held up my hand. "I can't do this anymore, all right? I can't keep telling myself that what I do makes any difference in this shithole place."

Baker was quiet.

I was afraid I was going to cry. "I'm tired," I said. "I'm tired, and I just feel so alone."

Baker still said nothing, just put the cruiser in gear and we moved slowly forward. I leaned my head back and closed my eyes.

I don't know how long I stayed like that, in a half-sleep state, lulled by the murmur of the radio and the movement of the cruiser. When I realized we had stopped, I opened my eyes.

We were in a deserted parking lot. The peeling white façade of Tiger Stadium loomed in the windshield. Baker was gone. Then I saw him coming toward the cruiser carrying two Styrofoam cups. He slid in and handed me a cup and a pack of Splenda.

For several minutes we sat in silence, sipping our coffees.

"My dad used to bring me here for games," Baker said, nodding to the stadium. "We were in the bleachers for the seventh game of the '68 series when Northrup hit a two-run rope into center to win. It was great."

"I wasn't even born then, Baker," I said.

He gave me a half-smile, set his coffee in the holder and put the cruiser in gear. We headed down Michigan Avenue, past empty office buildings with paper masking their windows. It had started to rain again, and in the distance I could see the gleaming glass silos of the Ren Cen.

Baker slowed and pointed to the abandoned Book-Cadillac building. "My mom took my sister and me to have tea there once," he said, nodding. "I guess she was trying to give me some class. I guess it didn't take."

I stared at the old hotel's boarded-up windows. There was a sign in one that said, FRIENDS OF THE BOOK-CADILLAC with a website for donations.

At Grand Circus Park, Baker swung the cruiser around the empty square and slowed as we moved unto the shadows of the People Mover overhead. "My dad used to bring us down here to the show," Baker said. "The Madison is gone now but the United Artist is still there. That's where I saw *Ben-Hur*."

I knew Baker had grown up in Detroit and that after his wife died fifteen years ago, he had sold their house in Royal Oak and moved back. But he had never before talked about the city and its deterioration.

Baker pulled to a stop at the curb. We were in front of the Fox Theater now. In the gloom of the afternoon rain, the ten-story neon marquee with its winged lions pulsed with lights. Tickets were on sale for *Sesame Street Live*.

"They almost tore this down, you know," Baker said. "But that millionaire pizza man bought it. Fixed it up, opened it back up and moved his office in upstairs."

I looked out at the empty street. "Why would anyone with half a brain invest in this place?"

"Maybe he couldn't stand to see one more good thing die," Baker said.

I stared at the winged lions. I heard Baker unhook his seatbelt and looked over.

He reached under his seat and came up with a crumbled brown paper bag, molding in a distinctive shaped that I recognized immediately.

He pulled the gun from the bag and handed it to me. It was an older S&W Model 10 revolver. The bluing was chipped along the barrel. The gun was clean but it had seen its share of street time.

"Remember me telling you about Hoffner?" Baker asked.

"Your first partner," I said. My mind flashed on the photograph of the jowly man on the memorial wall back at the Beaubian station. Shot to death in a drug bust.

"That was..." Baker paused, searching for the word he wanted. Cops had a way of doing that, selectively choosing words that could be interpreted one way by other cops and another more benign way by the rest of the world.

"Hoffner and me, we called that gun our third partner," Baker said.

I turned the weapon over. The serial number had been acid-burned away. But this gun was so old I doubted it had a registered owner anywhere. I knew why. Hoffner's gun was a throw-down, a handy way of fixing the worst mistake a cop could make – shooting an unarmed suspect.

"Did this partner ever have to do any work?" I asked.

"Not on my watch."

"Why are you giving it to me?"

"Because every officer should have one."

"And you think I might need it one day?"

"No," Baker said. "I think you need it now."

I need to know why. I need to know why they do it.

So, I find this book about lions and I read it, because I have this idea that if I can find out why they roar I can figure out a way to stop it.

I read about the lions of the Serengeti, how they have different sounds to mark their territories, to attract female lions, to find each other when they are separated, to call their cubs when they are lost.

But that awful group roaring that comes every night. What is that?

I read on.

When a strange male lion comes into a pride he kills all the cubs too small to escape him. He kills because it ends the mother lion's investment in her cubs and brings her back into fertility sooner.

But...

Sometimes the female lions band together and roar as a group to drive the killer male away. They roar as one to make sure their cubs survive.

That night, when the roaring builds to its crescendo, I lay there and listen. I listen, trying hard to interpret the sounds, trying hard to hear my own heart.

I was sitting in my personal car, Hoffner's old chipped gun on the seat next to me. I hadn't brought my service weapon or either of the other two guns I had locked up at home. I didn't want to take any chances that I would somehow screw it up and use the wrong one.

I had never worried about things like that before. Confusing guns or being seen somewhere I shouldn't be, or worrying about performing my duties in the way I had been trained. I was a professional.

But I had never killed someone before.

Not even in the line of duty. Until now, I had been grateful for that. But somewhere in the last few days, and more so in these last few hours spent sitting outside Angela's apartment building, I had the unforgiveable yearning to know what it felt like to kill.

I checked my watch. Nine p.m.

Angela had left earlier for her job, turning to blow a kiss to her teenage daughter who stood in the doorway holding the baby.

I was relieved that Angela had not left the baby alone with Streeter, but I was worried for the daughter.

I knew I couldn't go up there. I needed to be invisible now, to Streeter and to my fellow cops. I only hoped that I could make my move before Streeter made his.

If he made one.

My thoughts were shifting again, drawn to that basic human hope that men were not wild animals. And for that moment, I questioned what I was doing. But only for a moment, because this job had taught me different.

I checked my watch again. Nine-twenty.

A light went out in the apartment. I knew it was in Angela's bedroom and I let out a breath, thinking that Streeter was going to bed. I would have to wait. Wait and hope he didn't do anything.

I had just reached for the keys when the apartment door opened and Streeter hustled out. His leather jacket caught the orange beam of the streetlight before he disappeared into the darkness.

I started my car and followed slowly, hugging the curb but keeping my distance. He seemed intent on his destination, his pace quickening as he crossed the street and made a turn south. I though he was heading to the bar over on Woodward, but then he jagged east, head down, hands sunk deep into his jacket pockets. As he entered a block of abandoned houses, he slowed, looking to the structures as if he wasn't sure which one he wanted. I knew then what he was doing.

Out of prison three days and already sniffing out a new supplier.

He found it at the corner.

It was a listing shingle-sided house missing half its porch. The windows were boarded up but a faint light was visible behind a web of curtain in the small upper-story window.

Streeter stopped on the sidewalk, half-hidden behind a mound of trash. He stood in a glistening puddle of broken glass, his head swiveling in a nervous scan of the street. I had stopped halfway down the block and was slumped in the seat, confident my rusty Toyota didn't stand out in the ruins around us.

He went inside.

I waited.

He was out again in less than three minutes, hand in his pocket, unable to resist fondling the rock of crack as he walked. I slipped down in the seat but he didn't even look my way as he hurried past. He was already tasting his high. It would be the only thing on his mind.

I rose, and in my rearview mirror I watched his retreat. I started the car and eased away from the curb.

He was going home.

And I would get there before him.

In the few seconds before he arrived, I took small, calming breaths and I hoped for things I had no right to hope for.

I hoped that the T-shirt I had brought to put over the gun would muffle the sound. I hoped the people who lived here were too used to gunfire to hear it anymore. I hoped no one had seen me move from my car to the shadows at the side of the apartment building. I hope Angela would not grieve for this man too long.

I heard his footsteps before I saw him.

It kicked my heart up another notch and I drew what I knew would be my last full breath for the next few minutes.

I raise the gun. Kept it close to my side so it was partially obscured.

The sheen of his leather jacket caught the glow of the streetlight first. Then I saw a slice of skin and the glint of an eye that for a second looked more animal than human.

Two steps further and his entire body came into focus. He was walking straight toward me, but the emptiness of the night made me invisible to a man seeing only the weak yellow light of his front door.

He stopped at the stoop, nose and ears turned up to the air, as if he could smell my presence.

I stepped from the darkness.

I waited one second for my face to register in his brain because I wanted him to know who I was and why he had to die.

When I saw the fearful recognition in his eyes I fired. Once.

Trusting my ability to hit him in the heart. Knowing one shot would attract far less attention than six.

He fell straight down, his knees hitting the pavement with a bone-jammed thud. His hand went to his chest, and for a second he was frozen in that position, eyes locked open, blood pouring from between his fingers.

He fell face first with a fleshy smack to the concrete.

I made myself a cup of tea and took it to my bed. The television was on, the sound low but the light putting out something close to a comforting glow.

My hand trembled as I brought the cup up to my lips and took a drink.

There was nothing about Streeter on the 11 o'clock news but I knew there wouldn't be. A crack addict getting shot on a random Detroit street didn't merit a mention. Still, I watched.

The talking heads lobbed it over to sports. I hit the mute and leaned back on my pillows as the silence filled my small basement room.

I would go see Angela in a day or two. Give her enough time and space. Give myself enough time and space.

My head was pounding with fatigue. I set the cup aside and closed my eyes.

The ring of the phone jarred me awake. The TV was still on. I caught the green dial of the clock as I went for the receiver. Twelve-fifteen.

"Yeah, hello?"

"Detective Sheffield?"

The voice was deep but definitely female, with an authoritative calm that sent a small chill through me.

"Yes," I said.

"Detective, this is Lieutenant Janklow over at the Western District."

I felt my heart give an extra beat.

"We had a report tonight of a shooting in your district, a Curtis Streeter."

I closed my eyes.

"Detective Sheffield?"

"A shooting...yes."

"We know what you did."

I couldn't move.

"Don't worry, detective, you're not alone."

I brought a shaking hand up to my face.

"There are six of us now," the woman said. "The others asked me to call you and welcome you to our group."

There was a long silence on the other end of the line. Then the woman's voice came back, softer now.

"Good night, detective."

A click, then silence.

I opened my eyes. My hand was still shaking as I set the receiver back in its cradle.

Something wakes me. A sound in my dreams or something outside? I can't tell. I jerk awake, my eyes searching the darkness.

But it isn't really dark. There is a gray light in the corner of my room, creeping in from the edges of the window. I throw back the sheet and go to the window.

Not dawn. Not yet. Still night but almost there.

And then I hear it. The roaring. But it sounds different now, still edged with anger, still deep with pain. But now with a strong pulse of relentless strength. The lions will be quieted.

I go back to my bed. The sound is in my ears. I sleep.

"Lost and Found" was inspired by books like TRUE BLUE, a series of behind-the-badge stories written by Sgt. Randy Sutton, and some long and honest conversations with a veteran officer of the Memphis PD. Everyone knows that police work is hard, and with that each call and each case, it is possible to lose a piece of yourself. But is it also possible to find something?

LOST AND FOUND

He sat alone in the dark cruiser, staring out the window into the shimmering darkness. It was just starting to rain, more of a mist really, tiny glittery drops that seemed to fall from nowhere and disappeared before the hit the ground.

He turned off the wipers and after a few moments, the glass began to blur, the rain working like a slow silver paint brush to erase his view of the bridge and the man on it.

A.J. sighed softly. The car was a comforting cocoon of drifting shadows, blinking red radio lights, and the familiar hug of the old leather seat on his back.

There weren't many moments like this, so he held on to it for a while, another full minute, before he hit the wipers again. In the wet glow of the cruiser's headlights, the bridge, and the rookie standing on it, came back into focus.

The rookie was young, with an awkward bent-stick way of walking. His face, with his crooked Alabama smile, was eager, anxious and hopeful. Not a whole lot different than the last rookie A.J. had. Or the one before that. Or the one before that.

The bridge was old and plain, too big, really, for the trickle of brown water that flowed beneath it. The bridge's face, a stretch of bleached concrete, was chipped and scarred by too many drunks, and smeared in more recent years with red and yellow slashes of gang graffiti.

The bridge seemed to the only thing standing still in the drifting night. Maybe it was the distant city lights as they played off the underbelly of the low-hanging clouds. Or maybe it was the fog slithering around the rookie's feet. Whatever it was, it was the kind of night that held something A.J. had felt before. It was the kind of night that could crawl inside you and suck something out, something you couldn't see leaving but could feel.

A.J. glanced out the side window, his mind drifting with the trickles of water.

Lorraine liked these kinds of nights, but she never saw them like he did. He recalled her saying more than once, usually on one of their anniversaries that it had been raining like this – this weird glittery kind of mist — the night he proposed to her.

She had a word for this kind of night, but right now he couldn't remember that, either. What had she called it?

Londonesque. Yeah, that was it.

Must be what London is like, don't you think, A.J.? It's Londonesque. Do you think we could go there on our honeymoon, A.J.?

He never understood the word Londonesque but he never told her that. Never told her he didn't understand most of her fancy words. Didn't tell her he suspected she made some up.

They didn't go to London on their honeymoon. In fact, they hadn't gone anywhere on their wedding night. But Lorraine kept planning other "honeymoons" to other places. Places, like her made-up words, that she thought could make her someone or something else. Something smarter or prettier or better than what she was. A cop's wife.

A.J. had never been much farther than St. Louis, but for the moment, in this weather, and maybe because he was feeling a bit lonely lately, and a bit kindly toward Lorraine right now, he could imagine, if things had gone differently, that he and Lorraine might be in England. Strolling around of those old castles, taking pictures of those stiff-lipped, fuzzy-headed guys standing guard.

He sighed.

She'd been gone a long time now. Left him, married her dentist and moved to Knoxville, where he knew they had no castles but he guessed they had a few pink brick houses with big backyards. He didn't know where she lived now. Didn't know if she ever got to England.

A.J. looked back at the rookie on the bridge.

His name was Andy. The leather jacket squared off his shoulders, making it look tougher and beefier than A.J. knew he was under the stiff leather. Andy's blue trousers were knife-creased, and speckled with mud from the climb down and back up the hill. They were a might short, too, and every time Andy leaned forward on the bridge, A.J. could see a flash of his bright white tube socks.

Andy's eyes were a pale brown, the color of beach sand. Kind, trusting eyes, but eyes that held no sense of command. A.J. knew that people – bad people – noticed things like that. A nervous tic, a tremor in the voice, a wrong step in the wrong direction, trusting eyes, all those things that told a bad guy who was in charge.

Andy was going to have to lose the trusting look if he was going to survive.

A.J. shifted in his seat to ease the stiffness in his lower back and glanced at the clock, wondering where the detectives were. It was almost midnight, shift's end. Usually he could gauge the time pretty well without looking and he was surprised it was so late. He raised his hand to flickering computer screen to check his watch. The crystal was a little fogged and he blew on it to clear it. Sometimes that worked.

The watch was probably in its final days, but it had been a good watch, the kind a cop needed. Something that could get smacked against a wall, dropped in a lake, or even stepped on and still keep ticking, like that old commercial said. When it died, he wouldn't throw it away. He would lay it in his jewelry box, next to all his old service medals and outdated badges.

It had been his daughter Sheila's last gift to him, in June of 1998. He had thought it was a Father's Day gift until he saw it was wrapped in Christmas paper, left over from six months earlier when he hadn't shown up at the Knoxville house like he promised he would.

Sheila didn't understand too many things back then, like how long it took to remove crumpled cars, wet Christmas presents and dead bodies from a freeway exchange. She didn't understand that that ex-wives had their own reasons for not giving daughters messages from their father.

He supposed most sixteen-year olds didn't understand stuff like that. They saw the world only through their own selfish prisms and in their drama thought even the smallest thing could ruin their lives forever. His not showing up for that Christmas was that one small thing for Sheila.

He hadn't made it to Knoxville the following Christmas, either, but he had called and asked Sheila to come see him. The day before, she canceled, leaving a message on his answering machine that that she had other plans.

He tapped on his watch. The crystal was still clouded.

He wondered if Seikos clouded up. Probably not. Those beauties were sterling silver, emblazoned with the police department logo and inscribed with the officer's name on the back. They were given to officers after twenty-five years of service, presented in a satin-lined case by the chief at a ten minute ceremony the wives and kids could attend.

A.J. reached down and picked up a half-eaten Hershey bar off the console and broke off a square of chocolate.

The department had stopped giving the watches last November. Said they couldn't afford it anymore, what with all the recent pay increases, EEOC-mandated promotions, law suits on excessive force, worker's comp injuries and the high cost of computer, radar guns, patrol cars, tin badges and gasoline.

A.J.'s twenty-fifth anniversary was next month. He had mentioned that and the watch thing to Andy a few days ago and Andy had asked why he just buy a watch have it engraved to himself.

Don't you think it loses just a little meaning that way, kid?

He looked back at Andy, hitting the wipers to clear his view.

Suddenly Andy leaned over the railing and lost the rest of his country fried steak dinner into the river. He coughed a few times, drew himself tall and used a neatly folded handkerchief from his back pocket to wipe his mouth.

A.J. studied Andy's face. In the harshness of the cruiser's headlights, it was ghostly and pained. A.J. knew the ghost-like part came from what lay beneath the bridge. But the pained part, that was something else.

It was embarrassment, something A.J. understood. It was pretty undignified to puke in front of a senior officer, all over your new blue uniform and your just-out-of-the-box Rockports.

Maybe there was something that happened to men when they stood on bridges, like standing in the middle of a bridge put them half-way between something good and bad. Or weak or strong. Or between yesterday and tomorrow.

He had stood on a bridge once. A high arcing overpass near the airport. It had been his assigned ward back then – when was it? Nineteen eighty-six? Eighty-seven?

The ice storm had started about nine a.m. By nine-thirty, two cars had slid off the ramps onto the snowy embankments. A.J. had been sent to the bridge to monitor traffic, slow down speeders and call ambulances for idiots who thought they could still do sixty across an iced-over bridge fifty feet in the air.

He had a ride-along passenger that day, some woman from the neighborhood watch committee who the chief thought needed a tour of duty in order to see how hard the police were working on community relations.

It would have been a fine day, normally, with the ice storm a perfect setting to allow an epic display of police compassion. Except for the fact that A.J. had the beginnings of a flu as he started his watch on the bridge. The stomach cramps began around ten and by noon, he was covered in a suit of ice, his fingers so frozen he could barely key the radio to ask be briefly relieved.

The request was denied. Three times. The storm had stretched the department thin. He was needed, they said. There was no one else.

So he had toughed it out. Four hours, standing on the side of the overpass, waving his flashlight at the slow-moving headlights, his body shivering uncontrollably, and watery burning shit running down the back of his legs.

The neighborhood watch woman never asked what the smell in the cruiser was when he got back in. But there was that look of disgust in her eyes as they made their way back to the precinct, like she thought he was some sort of animal who was too lazy or too uncivilized to use the toilet like decent human beings do.

The chatter on the radio brought him back to the moment. Andy was still bent over the concrete wall, head in his hands. A.J. thought about going to him but decided not to. The kid would come back when he was ready.

A.J. reached over to turn up the heat. The fan rattled on and vent puffed out warm air.

He was adjusting the direction of the flow when, out of the corner of his eye, he caught a glimpse of a folded paper on the passenger floorboard. He picked it up and in the dim light, unfolded it. It was Andy's paycheck stub.

A.J. knew how much money rookies made. Because of the union, starting salaries were common knowledge, posted on the department's web site. But still, A.J. wanted to look.

Thirty-two thousand, one hundred and seventy-four dollars. Awful lot of money for a rookie who didn't know shit about what he was doing or why.

His gaze moved to the deductions.

A hundred buck automatic deposit to the First Bank of Tennessee. Union dues. Federal taxes. Social security. 401k contributions. Payroll deducted equipment costs. The kid had bought himself a second Kevlar vest.

A.J. looked to the dashboard, at the picture Andy had clipped there earlier tonight. The photo was of Andy's wife and baby. The woman, a wide-eyed beauty looked a lot younger than Andy, and the baby was so new it was still wrinkled.

He folded the check stub and set it on the seat. Thirty-two thousand was nowhere near enough.

A.J. made decent money now, decent enough, he guessed, for a single guy long past child support. But in the early years, when Lorraine was young and raising Sheila and trying to make a home for them, it had been a struggle. Later, after he lost track of Sheila, he started sticking almost a third of his paycheck into a savings account. He had found a nice little cabin on Lake Ark-abutla down in Mississippi and he wanted to buy it.

Eight grand into the plan, he met Spider Jackson, a trash talk-ing street germ with a big attitude and a bigger father who wielded one of the sharpest legal swords in the city and who had an iron-clad political connection, like being in-law related to the mayor's sister.

Spider had been caught red-handed selling stolen guns and, as all dirtbags do when they're high and scared, he resisted ar-rest. Bit a chunk of flesh out of one of the officer's hand, kneed another in the groin and sliced open the abdomen of a third be-fore he found himself in the back of a patrol car, alive but hurt-ing.

A.J. never hit Spider. Didn't get there in time to do anything except drive him to the jail and escort him inside. All the way, Spider was yelling about how he was going to sue everybody but A.J. had heard it all before and hadn't given the incident another thought until a few weeks later when his name showed up on a subpoena in a police brutality lawsuit.

The car was too warm now. A.J. turned off the heat and used his sleeve to wipe the condensation off the glass so he could keep an eye on Andy.

In the old days, people sued just the city. Nowadays, they could sue the officers, too, and that's what Spider's father did. In the end, the city settled their part of the lawsuit and the jury divided the balance of the settlement up among the officers.

Later, the lawyer explained to him that since all the officers denied any culpability, the jury had no reason to believe that A.J. was the only one who was really innocent. And besides, he said, you know better than anyone that to some people, you're all just white faces in blue uniforms.

The court took the eight thousand in one lump sum and set up a payment plan for the rest. His final payment was in August of this year.

A.J. reached down to pick up his coffee cup. His fingers had stiffened up again and he couldn't grab the cup the way most folks grabbed things, so he picked it up with his index finger and thumb, transferring it to his left hand to drink it.

He looked down at his hand. His pinkie finger was about gone, shot off by a punk armed robber firing blindly as he tumbled his way down a fire escape. The bullet had ripped through A.J.'s palm, mangling the tendons and severing the pinkie.

Another cop had been on the fire escape that day. His partner, dead from a bullet to the head, lying there on the black iron, his blue eyes open toward the sky, his gun still in his holster.

A.J. had seen it happen. But even now, he couldn't remember it well. All he could remember feeling at that moment was his pain and his fear and all those other selfish emotions that come when you think you're going to die.

He could remember the funeral a few days later. The long line of police cars crawling the freeway and the smell of white mums and the saddest damn music he had ever heard at a gravesite.

And he remembered the endless rows of uniforms, and the stiff, solemn faces looking at him from the other side of the flag-draped casket, silently wondering why two veteran cops hadn't been able to catch one sixteen-year-old dirtbag. Wondering why A.J. hadn't managed to fire off one single round from his weapon, because he was, they knew, the first one out the window. Wondering all that and never saying a word.

A.J. laid his head back against the seat and closed his eyes.

His dead partner had four ex-wives, but not one came to the funeral, so it had been A.J. who accepted the folded flag afterward. His wife Lorraine had put the flag on the top shelf of the closet. Said she put it there so she wouldn't have to look at it and be reminded every day just how suddenly she could become a widow, too.

Right after, the department had stuck him behind a desk in the traffic division, saying that because of his finger, he couldn't shoot accurately anymore. Maybe afraid, too, that he couldn't pull his gun quick enough to keep from getting shot himself. That year they had paid out over two hundred grand in widow's pensions and they couldn't afford any more.

He had stayed at the desk in the traffic division for over a year, slogging through paperwork. Every night he'd uncap the bottle of Jim Beam and try to tune out Lorraine's whining and find some peace. Finally, Lorraine told him that if he wanted some peace, she would give it to him. The next day she was gone.

A week later, when he was looking for his old revolver, he found the folded American flag among some Rolling Stones records. He stood there in his bedroom, holding it in his hands, thinking that he needed to find a place of honor for it, some place better than the top of a dusty closet.

He bought a triangular oak case and set the flag on the counter next to the bottle of Jim Beam. A few weeks later, the flag was still there. The bottle of whiskey wasn't. And he decided he wasn't going to replace it.

He practiced at the range for a month, always alone, too embarrassed to let anyone see his fumbling. Finally, he found enough agility in his left hand and enough confidence in himself to ask for another shot at requalifying. A week later, he was back behind the wheel of a cruiser.

That's when he finally understood what Lorraine felt, trapped in a life and feeling second rate, so invisible, that you plan honeymoons that are as elusive as the fog.

Londonesque. Maybe that's what she meant.

A calm female voice came from the radio. A.J. keyed his mike and acknowledged.

"Looks like the detectives are five minutes out," she said.

A.J. thanked her and clicked off.

Andy was leaning against the half-wall, staring out at the darkness. A.J. figured he was done throwing up and was now probably trying to unscramble things in his head. The trails of fog around Andy's feet disappeared. For a second, everything was clear add silent, as if the night was holding its breath.

Andy would be different in the morning, A.J. knew. He wouldn't know why, because he didn't understand yet that this was kind of moment that you lose a piece of yourself in, something taken away by that thing that crawls inside you and sucks something out, something you didn't miss for a long while. But one day, after a time, if he found himself sleepless and alone, he might wonder where it went and if he could get it back.

Andy let out a breath deep enough to raise his shoulders and turned and looked toward the cruiser. He was ready now.

A.J. pushed from the car and started across the bridge. Andy stepped forward. Under the streetlight, A.J. could see the rookie had his color back but his forehead was still beaded with sweat. Or rain. He lowered his eyes then, forced himself to look up.

"How you feeling?" A.J. asked.

When Andy found his voice, it was thick with the scorch of vomit. "Don't tell the guys I lost my dinner, okay?"

"Not a problem," A.J. said.

Andy's eyes drifted reluctantly back to the edge of the railing, then down toward the water, but he didn't move from his spot. He looked lost as to how he should behave or where he should keep his eyes. A.J. stepped forward and placed a hand on the wet concrete railing.

The inky water slithered through banks of thick brush, rocks and cypress trees. One of the trees had been shattered a lifetime ago by a bolt of lightning.

That's where she lay. In the arms of the dead tree.

Her name was Tammy.

They had gotten the missing person's report almost two weeks ago, just another thirteen-year-old girl with a juvenile record, a know-it-all attitude and a boyfriend who thought it was sexy to cover her neck in hickeys.

A.J. and Andy had been called to her house to take the initial report and he had let Andy take the lead. They had stood in the dirty cramped living room, Andy's pen poised over his notebook. The mother had been unable to remember much about her daughter, except that recently she had died her hair red, though she wasn't sure if it was still red now or some other color.

She didn't know the last names of any of her daughter's friends. She wasn't even sure if her daughter had attended school that day. Sometimes she skipped, the mother said.

Andy had stood there, looking down at an almost blank page in his notebook. Later, on the walk to the cruiser, Andy had turned and looked back at the house.

It was like she was lost long before she was lost, Andy had said

Then, the mother had come to the porch, calling to them, offering one last recollection.

"Hey officers...she had this T-shirt she loved, something with rhinestones on the front that said Too Hot To Handle. She's probably wearing that."

A.J. pulled back from the bridge railing and pulled out his flashlight. He shined it down into the blackness below. In the thin beam of light, the T-shirt looked more like a rag, the fabric eaten away by eleven days of cold, rushing water. The collar hung loose around a blackened, decomposing neck.

For a second, A.J. thought he could see the glint if rhinestones, but he knew he must be wrong. The stones would be moldy now, if they were even still there.

The T-shirt was the only piece of clothing on her body.

Andy came up beside him and stared down to the body.

"Not going to get sick on me again, are you?" A.J. asked.

"No, sir," Andy said, drawing a deep breath. "It gets easier the third and fourth time."

A.J. clicked off the flashlight. "It never gets easier."

They both turned away from the body. In the distance, A.J., could hear a siren and knew that in a few minutes, the road would be lit with lights.

"If it doesn't get any easier," Andy said, "how does anyone do this for twenty-five years?"

"You just find ways," A.J. said. "And things I guess."

"Things like what?" Andy asked.

A.J. was quiet for a moment, not sure why he had said it, and now at a loss to come up with any one thing that made this job bearable for twenty-five years. Except maybe some good bourbon. And he thought about offering that tidbit of veteran wisdom to the kid, telling him to just pack up and get out now before he ended up with an ex-wife, an entire city that hated the sight of him, a sotted liver and one less finger.

But he didn't say any of that.

"You find things like her," A.J. said, gesturing to the side of the bridge.

"But she's dead, sergeant," Andy said. "How is finding her a positive thing?"

"Because we didn't have anything to do with how she got to being dead," A.J. said. "But we got everything to do with what happens to her now. Now she gets to go home. And when you find the value in that, that's how you do this for twenty-five years."

"Will we get any recognition for finding her?"

"No," A.J. said.

Andy thought about that for a minute, then took the flashlight from A.J.'s hand. He shined it back down into the tree limbs, holding it on the pink shirt for a long time. From the brush, the chirr of crickets started up.

"Then I want to remember this moment," Andy said. "I don't ever want to forget t."

"You won't."

Andy set the flashlight down, pointing it so the beam ran along the top of the concrete half-wall. He drew a pocketknife from his pocket and flipped it open.

"What are you doing?" A.J. asked.

Andy squatted and started carving in the concrete. A.J. glanced down the road for the cruisers, then back at Andy. Andy's blade was scraping furiously.

The first headlights were coming down the road when Andy brushed away the gray dust and put his knife back in his pocket. Then he walked off to meet the approaching cruiser.

A.J. picked up the flashlight and shined it down on what Andy had written.

I FOUND TAMMY. BADGE #221.

A.J. looked back Andy as he walked down the bridge. His steps were more sure, his shoulders more squared.

A.J. turned back at the crude carving in the concrete. Then slowly, struck with a strange compulsion to write something, he pulled out his own pocketknife and worked the rusty blade open.

I FOUND...

He paused, the blade poised over the concrete, the cold wind pushing at his back, the wail of sirens growing closer.

I FOUND...

No words came to him, no lightning bolt of inspiration, no grand epiphany of what this strange world of protecting and serving his world was all about.

He slowly folded his knife. Maybe he couldn't write anything because he didn't know those fancy, writerly words that people like Lorraine knew.

Or maybe it was just because there was nothing to write. Maybe he had never found anything worth writing about.

Or maybe he hadn't found it...yet.

A.J. slipped his knife back into his pocket and brushed away the dust from the two words he had carved, then turned and started walking toward bright, white glare of headlights coming onto the bridge.

When Joe Konrath asked us to con-
tribute to his anthology, we asked
what the theme was. Most anthologies
have one – the Akashic Noir series are
all centered on a geographic place, the
Mystery Writers of America every
year publishes a collection tailored to
a specific topic. Joe said, "Write about
a hit man." While most of our fellow
contributors – David Morrell, Law-
rence Block, Jeff Abbott – created

monsters, we created two losers who couldn't shoot straight. Even
in a bowling alley.

GUTTER SNIPES

The neon was a splash of red in the oily puddles of the asphalt, and every time a car went by it sent the red quivering.

It looked just like Helen's mouth, he thought.

Moon Renfro tossed his butt out the window and leaned back in the seat. He didn't need to be thinking about Helen. There was too much other stuff he needed to be using his brain for right now and there was just no extra space for trying to figure out what the hell he had done this time to set those lips of hers flapping again.

The neon sign was making this annoying buzzing sound. He looked up at it.

PAUL STROFFMAN'S LUCKY STRIKE

A couple of the letters were flickering, getting ready to die. He stared at the sign in admiration. It was original, put up there in the '60s when Paulie "Sour Kraut" Stoffman bought the place. It was big and flashy and when it was working right, a neon ball would roll across the top of the letters, knock down the pins at the end, and the red letters STRIKE would turn to yellow. The sign never worked right since back in '79, but then the city passed some dumb-ass ordinance so Paulie couldn't replace it even if he could afford to. So it kept breaking and Paulie just kept trying to fix it.

It was a fucking work of art after all. They didn't make 'em like that anymore.

Just like the Lucky Strike. Moon had to admit the place wasn't much to look at on the outside. Just a brick slab in a dying strip mall. But inside...

Paulie kept the insides up real good, kept the lanes oiled with the best stuff, and stripped them down twice a year instead of once a year. Had the best computerized scoring program that not only marked your score but flashed these cartoons of grinning turkeys and pins being sucked to dust. Things that really made you feel good about what you had just done.

Moon had been bowling at the Lucky Strike every Tuesday and Thursday nights for ten years and he loved it. Love the sharp smell of acetone, beer and smoke. Loved the constant clattering of the wood. Loved the feel of that old bowling shirt on his back and the idea that only four other guys in the world had ones just like it.

It was his life, and for ten years it had been a good life, one that provided him with friends, beer and even sex from the alley kittens who worked the snack bar. But best of all, he was somebody here. He carried the second highest average in the house, a 239. Only Bulldog Baker had a high one at 240.

Moon sucked on his cigarette.

One damn pin.

It started to drizzle so he cranked up the window halfway. He exhaled and watched the smoke swirl in the clammy air of the truck. His eyes were locked on the front door of the bowling alley and his insides were churning as he considered what he was about to do.

He had gone over every detail in his head, thought about every angle, asked himself every question. Well, every question but one: Did he have the balls to really go through with this?

A sudden noise made him jump. The neon sign was spitting and flickering. He leaned forward and looked up at the sign.

PAUL STROFFMAN'S LUCKY STRIKE

Then, suddenly, with a loud pop! Some of the letters were gone. Moon stared through the wet windshield at the sign, frowning. He switched on the wipers.

U MUST RIKE

His mouth fell open and he had to grab at his crotch to slap away the cigarette. He found the butt on the floor mat and then swung back up to look at the sign again. Damn. The letters were still there, big as life against the black sky. U Must Strike? Shit...it was a sign. It had to be. If he had been having any doubts before this, he didn't anymore.

The clatter of the falling pins drew his eyes back to the entrance of the bowling alley. A guy had come out and was slinking across the lot.

Moon stuck a hand out the window. "Shaky!"

Shaky Cruthers slumped toward Moon's car. He opened the passenger door and climbed inside, flipping his stringy black hair like a wet dog.

"Watcha doing here, Moon?" Shaky asked. "You didn't bowl tonight, did you?"

"No," Moon said. "I came to talk to you."

Shaky pulled a crumpled pack of Camels and matches from his shirt pocket, lit his cigarette and settled into the seat, drawing one knee up. "So, whatcha want?" he asked.

"I want to win the championship for the Triple J Doubles," Moon said. "I want that thousand dollars prize money and that trophy."

Shaky laughed. He had a weird laugh, like one of those little dolls with the talking strings in their necks. "You better run that by Bulldog first," he said.

Moon almost reached out and choked Shaky for his bad joke, but he didn't want to piss him off right now. But he did throw him a sneer and Shaky mumbled an apology.

"Hell, we're in good shape," Shaky said. "We're tied for first."

"But we've been sucking hind tit most of the year," Moon said. "We got only next week. I want you to do something for me."

"Anything, Moon."

"I want you to make sure we win."

Shaky almost laughed again, but he caught Moon's eyebrow slant and he sucked the laugh back in. "What do you want me to do? Stand down there and blow the pins down?"

"I want you to fuck with Bulldog."

Shaky choked on the cigarette smoke. His hacking filled the truck and Moon looked away, out to the darkness to tune him out.

"You done?" Moon asked finally.

"Yeah," Shaky gagged. "But man, I thought you was serious there for a minute."

"I am serious."

"Bulldog is as big as a damn semi, Moon. How am I supposed to fuck him up?"

"Not him, asshole," Moon said. "His equipment."

Shaky stared at him. Moon could see the reflection of the neon sign in his brown eyes.

"Listen," Moon said, "Bulldog bought a pair of Kangaroo Ultras at the beginning of the season. Second week he wore those shoes, he bowled a 300. He calls them his magic slippers."

"So?"

"I want you to steal them just before we start. It'll mess up his head."

"What? How?"

"It'll be easy," Moon said. "Before practice, Bulldog always goes in the bar to get his Rum and Coke and play the poker machine. That's when you steal his shoes."

"Why don't you do it, Moon?" Shaky asked, tossing his cigarette butt out the window.

"Because it would be bad karma for me to do it," Moon said. "You know how important karma is in bowling. I'd be plagued with ten pins for the rest of my life."

Shaky fell quiet, picking at his fingers, trying to pull of the little pieces of rubber left from his thumb tape.

Moon looked down at his cigarette, trying to decide if he could get one more puff out of it. It was important to get all the puffs you could, just like it was important to always get one of the pins of the 7-10 split because that's what a lot of games came down to. And a lot of averages, too. One damn pin.

Moon slid a glance to Shaky. "I'll give you my old Red Inferno ball," he said.

"That ball's got so many potholes it rolls down the alley like a moon rock," Shaky said.

"Okay, what then?"

"Man..."

Moon finished the cigarette and tossed it out the window. "Okay, the Inferno and my Brunswick three-baller bag. But you'll have to fix the right wheel. It keeps falling off."

Shaky pulled a long string of thumb tape from his hand and starting rolling it between his fingers. When he had it into a tiny ball, he tossed it out the window.

"What about your Atomic Revolution?" he asked. "Can I have that?"

"No fucking way," Moon said. "I worked three weeks OT to get that damn ball. It's a friggin' two-hundred-dollar piece of art. No way. No way."

"Buy a new ball with the prize money," Shaky said.

Moon shook his head again, trying to find his Camels. His hands were trembling so badly he couldn't pull one out and when he finally did, he broke it.

"I got other bills to pay," Moon said, ripping open the pack. "I'm two months behind on my mortgage and one month on this truck. And Helen's bitching at me to get her a new washing machine. I can't afford to give you my good ball and buy another one."

Shaky was still staring at his fingers and Moon finally tossed the cigarette pack to the dash and grabbed Shaky's collar, jerking him toward the windshield.

"See that up there?" Moon said.

"What?"

"The sign," Moon said, pointing up. "See the sign? Don't you get it? It's telling us something. It's telling us to strike."

Shaky blinked up at the sky. "Yoo...moo...sttt...kee?" he said slowly.

Moon tapped the windshield. "No, you moron, can't you read? You...Must...Strike. It's talking about Bulldog."

Shaky's eyes widened. "Wow," he whispered.

They both stared at the sign for a few moments then Shaky slumped back against the seat. His eyes stayed glued to the flickering neon.

"Just steal the shoes, huh?" he said. "That's all I have to do?"

"That's all you have to do."

It rained on position night, like it did most nights in May in Memphis. For some teams, the downpour would mean a forfeit since half the streets would be flooded and most bowlers – those that didn't have a true heart – would stay home. After all, the league was ending and if you weren't one of the top teams, you were already a loser anyway, so why risk your life driving through a lake just to win games no one cared about?

Moon was sitting at one of the tall back tables, a beer in his hand, his eyes scanning the emptiness. Moon couldn't imagine not showing up every week, rain or sleet. It was being a purist was all about.

He hadn't known that until a few years ago, when in a drunken bar conversation, the pro shop guy Al "The Hawk" Hawkins, had first called Moon a purist. Moon had gotten mad until he looked up purist in the dictionary and realized The Hawk had paid him a helluva a compliment.

Shaky had a good heart but he wasn't a purist. Like his average. For as long as Moon had known him, Shaky had never gotten above a 199, and he seemed content to let that one pin stay beyond his reach, like there was absolutely no difference between a 199 and a 200 average.

Now Bulldog Baker. He's wasn't even close to a purist.

Yeah, he wore the silver Dyno-Thane Kangaroo Tour Ultras, and a glove called a Power Paw, and had made a name for himself a few years back by throwing a ball called The Thing. One day, The Thing had cracked in half on its way to the seven pin, only because Bulldog hadn't respected it enough to take it out of his car trunk all summer. Bulldog tried to get another Thing but it was out of stock, so he bought The Thing's new version — a purple and orange monstrosity called The Thing Lives.

Jesus. Having a ball with a stupid name was bad enough. But Bulldog also like to act the fool out there, sometimes wearing a dog mask or bowling with his eyes closed, or clipping a rubber chicken to his teammate's ass and then laughing like hell as it swung and bounced during the guy's approach.

You didn't do stuff like that in league.

Moon took a drink and spun his chair to look around. On the wall above the alleys was another version of PAUL STROFF-MAN'S LUCKY STRIKE sign. Moon stared at it for moment, waiting for a message, but he knew none would come. This sign was newer and not the classic symbol the one outside was.

A few dripping bowlers were straggling in. Tony Valleni, who had memorized every page of the ABC rule book. And Bald Leo, whose thumb was sliced off a few years back but who had worked real hard to learn to throw a curve using just his two fingers in the holes. True hearts at their best.

At five-thirty-seven Bulldog came through the front door, lugging his rain-speckled bag. Bulldog always carried two balls with him — The Thing Lives and a second ball he used only for spares. After he was done hugging the girls, shaking hands with the guys and talking about last night's scores, Bulldog made his way toward alleys eleven and twelve. He had small, penny-colored eyes pressed in a catcher's mitt of a face and they glinted with something Moon read as victory, even though not a ball had been thrown yet.

"You're here early," Bulldog said. "What, you soaking up the atmosphere for inspiration?"

Moon drew hard on his cigarette and just stared.

Bulldog gave him a smile then set his bag against the rack that held the ugly pink and green house balls. He glanced up at the computerized scoreboards. The team names were already up there. THE STEEL BALLS VS. BULLDOG'S BEST.

"I didn't know we were playing you guys," Bulldog said,

"It's friggin' roll-off night," Moon said dryly.

"Good Lord," Bulldog said with a wink. "Is the season almost over already?"

Moon snubbed out his cigarette, crunching his teeth to avoid saying anything that would get him punched. Besides, he needed to stay focused right now.

Bulldog unzipped his bag and pulled out The Thing Lives and started toward the ball return to place it on the rack. Moon gaped. Bulldog was going to walk on the polished approach with wet shoes.

"Hey!" Moon called. "Watch it! Your shoes are wet!"

Bulldog looked down at his black work shoes then came back to his bag. He set The Thing Lives back inside then bent to untie his shoes.

"My apologies, Moon," he said. "Last thing I'd want is some-one sticking on the approach and getting hurt on my account."

Bulldog took off his shoes. Then, to Moon's surprise, he pulled out his Kangaroo Ultras and started to put them on.

He was putting on his shoes now...before he went to the bar. Shit! Shit!

"You gonna walk around this place in your bowling shoes?" Moon asked. "They'll get soaked."

Bulldog unzipped a pocket on the bag and held up a limp pair of red slip-on shoe covers. "Have no fear, my friend," he said, "I always use protection."

Then he laughed, that horrid hoarse chuckle that always sounded like he had a rag caught in his throat. He was still laughing as he pulled the slip-ons over his Kangaroos and sauntered off to the bar.

Moon couldn't stand it, couldn't sit still, and he pushed away from the counter so fast he almost tipped his beer. Winding his way between the bowlers, he shoved open the front door and stepped outside.

Shit! Fuck! Motherfucker! Tits!

How could he have been so stupid? Why didn't his keep his mouth shut about Bulldog's street shoes? Why couldn't he just let some stuff go instead worrying about a few drops of water getting on the approach?

Because you can't, he thought. It's who you are. You're a purist.

The red neon of the sign cracked and buzzed, drawing his eyes upward to the gray sky. Moon stepped out from under the overhang and look up. Different letters were struggling to stay aglow in the rain. Suddenly, the sign steadied itself and a handful of letters grew bright and solid.

T OFF LUC

Moon squinted into the rain. A new message.

Toff luc? Tough luck?

He stared harder, waiting for something else, waiting for the sign to show him the rest, tell him what to do now. But the letters just stood there, tall and fuzzy and red in the mist.

Tough luck. Tough luck. Tough luck.

Moon spat on the ground. This was bullshit. The sign wasn't some mystical crystal ball that was going to help him beat Bulldog and light the way for the re-purification of the greatest game ever invented. It was just a rusty old relic of a vanishing era.

He reached for the door. The boom of a blown electrical transformer made him snap his head back toward the sign. With a groan and a crackle, three new letters came to life.

T OFF LUC TRI

The last three – TRI – were blinking on and off.

TRI? Try? Try...that was it. Try. Try. Try!

Moon looked up to the clouds, his heart swelling with wonder and gratitude. He eyes filled with tears.

"You okay, Moon?"

Moon jumped then looked at the man who had spoken. It was Al "The Hawk" Hawkins, the pro shop guy. Moon's eyes slid back to the sign but he knew The Hawk couldn't read it.

"I'm cool," Moon said.

The Hawk motioned to his van. "I had to close the pro shop early. My old lady's in labor again. Good luck tonight, Moon. Seven years in a row coming in second place. That's gotta hurt after a while."

Moon couldn't even fake a smile. The Hawk hurried off across the parking lot. After a few seconds, a yellow Camaro swung in. Shaky was here.

Moon waited under the overhang until Shaky was almost to the doors then he stopped him with a palm to his chest.

"What? What's wrong?" Shaky asked.

"He's already wearing the shoes," Moon said. "You got to do something else."

"Like what?"

"Go to my truck. Inside the back is a full tube of epoxy. Bring it to me and don't let anyone see you with it."

"Huh?"

"Just go get it. I'll explain inside."

Moon pushed him out into the rain. Shaky planted his feet, blinking like he was trying to figure something out. "I do something with the epoxy then you gotta give me something better than your old Red Inferno," he said.

"What?" Moon demanded. "What the hell else I got you want?"

"A roll with Helen?"

"What? She'd never sleep with you."

"Get her drunk enough she might."

Moon came out from under the overhang, fist clenched, and Shaky backpedaled. "I was just kidding, man!"

Moon stopped himself, and for a few second, both of them stood in the rain, silent. Moon sighed. Man, he had to give Shaky something better than the pitted Inferno. Shaky didn't have much in his life. Hell, maybe the thrill of winning this was enough. Maybe Helen's new washer could wait.

"All right," Moon said. "I'll give you my Atomic Revolution."

In the gray mist, Shaky's eyes lit up like headlights. He loped off toward Moon's truck. A minute later, he was back.

"You get it?" Moon asked.

Shaky padded his wet shirt, his voice low. "I'm packing, man."

It was crowded by the time they got back to alley eleven. Beefy men hunched over black bowling bags. Shoes scattered everywhere. Counters covered with fine white powder from tiny bags of Easy-Slide. Paulie had music playing from the speakers, the kind Moon knew would give him a headache if he listened to it too long.

They had both dried off in the john, changed into their yellow and black shirts, and Shaky had opened the epoxy inside the stall, making sure it would be warm and ready when he needed it. He was only going to get one good squeeze per hole.

Back at alley eleven, Moon provided the cover for Shaky. He heard Shaky unzipping Bulldog's bag.

"Good luck tonight, Moon!" someone called.

Moon gave the man a tight nod, keeping his eyes on the alleys. The smell of epoxy was everywhere.

"Hurry up," Moon hissed to Shaky.

"Do you want I should do the spare ball, too?"

"Yeah."

Moon heard the draw of a zipper and then Shaky appeared in front of him, a tight smile on his face. "Mission accomplished."

Moon watched as Shaky wandered off and dropped the epoxy tube into a trash can then he looked toward the bar. Bulldog was coming out the door.

It was time to get ready.

As Moon put on his shoes, he snuck at look at Bulldog. He hadn't touched his bag yet. Still busy jawing about his recent 300 game and wondering when his award ring would come from ABC.

Moon's eyes slipped quickly to the only ring on his own hand, his wedding band, but he didn't like thinking about that. He set his Atomic Revolution on the rack and looked down at the pins. They stood like polished teeth at the end of the gleaming wood tongue.

"Who's been fucking with my ball?"

Bulldog had pulled The Thing Lives from his bag and was jabbing at the thumb hole with his finger. "It's...filled with something."

Moon resisted the urge to walk over. Bulldog poked at the clogged hole a few more times then his copper eyes came up. Right at Moon.

"You," Bulldog whispered.

Moon gave him a dry smile. "Things happen to balls when you leave them in car trunks," he said. "Maybe it melted."

Bulldog stared at him, The Thing Lives cradled in his hands like a dead pet.

People started to gather around, taking turns sticking fingers in Bulldog's thumbhole and mumbling about how the new kind of resin used to make ball nowadays just didn't hold up very well in the southern heat.

"Maybe Al the Hawk can drill it out for you real quick," someone said.

Moon let Bulldog take a few steps toward the pro shop before he called out, "Hey, Bulldog, I saw Al leaving about thirty minutes ago."

Bulldog turned slowly back to Moon. The mumbling around them grew louder. Everyone knew what this meant.

"You wanna borrow one of my balls, Bulldog?" someone asked,

"You know I can't," Bulldog said. "I got fat fingers."

"Maybe you can use one of those pink house balls," Moon offered.

Bulldog glared at him, so hard he didn't even notice that Bald Leo had walked up.

"Man, that's tough luck," Leo said. "Want me to teach you how to throw it without sticking your thumb in?"

Bulldog's head jerked to Bald Leo. "Yeah," he said quickly. "Show me."

They were allowed fifteen minutes of practice. With only two on a team, that gave everyone a chance to throw at least twenty shots. Normally, Moon took every one he could, but not tonight. He was watching Bulldog.

At first, Bulldog threw a couple of gutters then Bald Leo worked on Bulldog's grip, showing him how to cup the ball to get it to stay on his hand. Eight practice balls later, The Thing Lives, with the clogged holes, was rolling down the alley and getting strikes.

Moon was pissed. No one could learn to bowl with two fingers that quick. In fact, unless you were thumb-less, there ought to be a law against it. They put three holes in a ball for a reason.

"This sucks," Shaky said, coming up next to him. "What now?"

Moon's gut was so hard he couldn't speak. He shoved Shaky aside and ripped into his bag for his shoe covers. He was still struggling to get them on as he hobbled away from the alleys.

Moon shoved open the front doors and stepped out into the mist, looking up at the sign. Every damn letter was off.

"Okay!" Moon shouted. "Okay! Now what? What do I do now?"

The sign was silent and dark.

"Dammit!" he screamed. "I did everything you wanted me to! Talk to me. C'mon, one more time!"

Nothing.

"You lousy, stinking piece of cheap neon! Talk to me!"

It started with a buzz then came a crackle and a few letters began to glow. First a K, then a second K.

"C'mon," Moon said, "I'm running out of time here!"

More letters. Then the sign stopping buzzing, leaving only a handful of letters lit.

MAK SIK

What did that mean?

Ma...Make? S...i...k...Sick.

Make sick.

Yes! that was it! He would make Bulldog sick.

Moon rushed back inside, dripping all the way back to alley twelve. The whole place was alive now with clatter, but to Moon it seemed strangely muted, like it did sometimes at the end of a one-pin game when he had to tune everything else out in order to throw the perfect ball.

Bulldog was humping strikes every time now and his team-mates stood in awe watching him. Everyone was watching him.

Moon grabbed Shaky's sleeve and pulled him over to the counter.

"Get your acetone," he whispered.

Shaky reached down into his bag and pulled out a small plastic squeeze bottle. Moon glanced at the crowd around Bulldog then tipped his head toward Bulldog's Rum and Coke.

"Pour some in there," he said.

"You want me to poison him?" Shaky said.

"He won't die," Moon said. "He'll just get sick."

"I dunno, Moon, this is bad stuff."

"Just do it!" Moon hissed.

Shaky took the cap off the bottle then hesitated. "I want a bigger payoff," he said.

"You already got my Revolution. I ain't got nothing else!" Moon said.

"But I could go to jail for this."

Moon looked up, his throat tight. Behind him, he heard the smash of a strike – they made a clatter noise all their own — followed by laughter. Man, could he really do this? Yes, he could. He would make it up to her somehow.

"Okay," he said, looking back at Shaky. "If you want Helen — and I mean for one quickie — I'll get her to do it."

Shaky's eyes widened then he slurped the acetone into the drink and quickly put the bottle away. The scoreboards suddenly turned a bright blue, indicating practice was over. Everyone started back to their own lanes. Moon looked at Bulldog.

He was standing by the approach, holding The Thing Lives in his arm. He made a sweeping gesture toward the lanes.

"You're up, Moon."

Bulldog threw up in the wastebasket in frame nine of the first game, and no one was sure if he was going to be able to continue. But right after, he got back up and threw another strike — a Moses ball — the type that hits the head pin and divides the other pins right down the middle.

It was the kind of thing that always happened to unpure bowlers when they found themselves up against real talent. Moon called them ugly strikes, the ones that never should have been, and although everyone took them — you had to take them — Moon thought there was an element of shame in having too many. Bulldog didn't seem to think so.

Moon glanced up at the scoreboard. Dammit, they were going to lose this game. Shaky wasn't concentrating. His shots were laden with guilt and he was having a hard time keeping his eyes off Bulldog's drink.

Shaky apologized five times for losing the game, even though he had bowled a 218, nineteen pins above his average. Moon had bowled a 266. Any other night, it would have been more than enough. But not tonight.

Bulldog spent most of the second game in the bathroom. Moon wanted to called Tony Valleni and his rule book down to see if there was a set number of minutes someone could delay before they forfeited. But half the league was in the john, worried about Bulldog, and Moon didn't want to come off as a jerk. So he stayed quiet, just sitting at the table staring at the scoreboard, which by the end of the second game read: THE STEEL BALLS 521, BULLDOG'S BEST 499.

The series was even up. All they needed to do was win the third game and the championship, the thousand dollars, and that big-ass trophy would be his.

Moon rubbed his face, wishing the knot in his belly would go away. He looked out at the lanes. Most of the bowlers had stopped their games to gather behind eleven and twelve to watch the championship. The alleys were so quiet Moon could hear his own heart.

Someone called his name and he looked to see Bulldog and his entourage coming back to the alleys. Bulldog's fat face was sweaty and as white as the pins, and he was walking unsteady, but he managed to find his way to the approach and grab The Thing Lives.

Shaky started out the third game with a Moses ball strike. Moon followed with a perfect pocket hit, but so did Bulldog and his partner. By the middle of the game, amidst rolls of thunder and flickering lights, the game was tied, with X's in every box on the scoreboard. The crowd behind was thickening.

By the ninth frame, Bulldog was staggering, with only the cheers of the faithful to give him strength. Moon looked up at the scoreboard. They were a few pins behind but it was not out of reach. He was calculating how many pins he would need if Bulldog got a final strike when he heard a groan from the crowd and looked up.

Bulldog had done the unthinkable. The Thing Lives was rolling down the gutter.

Moon watched the ball until it disappeared into the black abyss behind the pins then his eyes flicked up to the scoreboard. His brain worked like lightening and he knew all he had to do was get a spare. Two balls to get all ten pins! It was theirs. Dammit, the whole thing was theirs!

Bulldog lofted his final ball, a weak hook that toppled the pins in slow motion. Holding his gut, he stumbled back to his chair and into the arms of his friends.

It was time to end this.

Moon picked up his Atomic Revolution and took his place on the approach. Lowering his head and concentrating on every step, he threw his first ball. It was perfect — absolutely friggin' perfect — and he felt a surge of greatness as the Revolution exploded into the pins and scattered them.

Wait...there was one left. One damn pin, the ten pin. The fucking damn ten pin, sitting there like it had been glued on the alley.

Dammit. Dammit to hell.

Moon grabbed the Revolution off the return and cradled it, staring at the ten pin. If he missed this, it was over. Everything was over.

He set himself, his heart starting to pound, beads of sweat forming on his palms. Just as he started his first step, thunder rolled overhead. Moon stopped, waiting for it to pass before he positioned himself again.

He wiggled his fingers into the ball, then slipped in his thumb and stared down at the pin. As he took a step, another explosion from outside vibrated through the building, sending the lights flickering and the ten pin trembling. Moon stopped again and stepped back.

The sign outside must have been flickering, too, trying to talk to him, and he wanted to go out to see what the message was but he couldn't leave now.

But then, suddenly, imaginary letters started flashing in his head. They made no sense, like one of those scrambled word puzzles in the newspaper that he could never do.

He set himself again, trying not to think about the letters but now words were forming in his head and with every step he took, another letter dropped into place.

S...T...A

Third step and the swing of his arm.

Y...P...

It amazed him that he could see his message now in his mind and that realization, more than the letters themselves, filled him with a sense of magical power as his arm started forward.

U...R...

The ball was cupped in his hand like a perfect size DD boob, and as he started to lay it down, the last letter dropped into place in his head.

E.

In an instant, he saw it, all the letters blinking as sure and strong in his head as he knew they were blinking outside.

STAY PURE

What the fuck? That wasn't the right message. It couldn't be the right message. He was already pure.

Wasn't he?

The Atomic Revolution was just coming off the tips of his fingers when something pulled at him, something powerful and creepy and irresistible, and he did something he never thought he would do. He flipped the ball just a half-inch to the left. The moment the ball hit the wood, he knew it would miss the pin.

And it did.

The ball disappeared into the black bowels of the alley, bringing a gasp from the crowd.

Moon stared at the ten pin.

It stared back, defiant.

Somewhere in his brain, he could now hear cheering and then the rattle of the Atomic Revolution coming up the ball return. But everything he expected to feel — rage and disappointment — none of it was there. All that was there was a scary kind of peace.

He turned and went slowly back to the bench. As he packed up his stuff, Shaky was talking about next year and Bulldog was shaking hands and someone was on the loudspeaker announcing that Bulldog's Best were league champs. From the corner of his eye, Moon caught sight of the huge gold trophy coming through the crowd.

He headed outside, Shaky hustling along behind him, still yakking about next year and summer leagues and tournaments. But Moon wasn't hearing him. He wanted to see the sign and he wanted to make sure the message he had seen in his head was the right one because if it wasn't, then everything that had happened to him in those last few seconds had been fake.

He stopped under the overhang and told Shaky to shut up. They both stepped out and stood there, staring up at the sign, watching and waiting.

With a crack of thunder, all the lights went out. A few seconds later, they began to flicker back on.

U L

U L O

U L O S R

Moon stared, and blinked, and kept staring. Then he started slowly off across the parking lot. Shaky trailed behind.

"Do I still get your Atomic Revolution, Moon?"

"No."

"What about Helen?"

"No."

"Well, what about your old red Inferno?"

"No."

"Well, then, what do I get out of all this, Moon?"

Moon stopped and faced him. "Purity, my friend. We get purity."

We're often asked where we get our ideas. The idea for this story grew from Kris's interest in the Florida panthers but when we wrote it, we realized there wasn't enough plot to go around. Some stories are like that. Some need 400 pages, others need only 40. So this is a novella that bridges Louis's time from the end of THE LITTLE DEATH to the beginning of HEART OF ICE.

CLAW BACK

A Louis Kincaid Novella

To our sexy beasts
Pearl, Bailey, Phoebe and Archie

CHAPTER ONE

He hadn't been inside in a long time.

It was as dark as he remembered, and it smelled as bad.

O'Sullivan's was a cop bar. Located a block from the Fort Myers police station, it had the feel of a married guy's den. Stale smoky air, cigarette burns on the tables, rows of trophies, a floor of crushed peanut shells and a big-screen TV permanently tuned to ESPN.

Like all primitive habitats, it had a pecking order. City detectives had staked out the back of the bar. County detectives, out of legendary necessity, owned the tables by the men's room so they could piss and moan more conveniently. The round tables in the middle belonged to the rank and file uniforms.

And in the back, by the juke box, sat Lance Mobley. Arms spread across the back of the booth, perched under a Happy Birthday banner, he looked like a king on a red leather throne.

Louis Kincaid waited until his eyes adjusted before he started back. He needed to see everything clearly right now because this wasn't going to be easy.

When he stopped at the table, Mobley was talking over his shoulder to a pretty lady in a blue halter top. No one was sitting in the booth with the sheriff, but the table was littered with empty bottles, heaping ash-trays and crumpled wrapping paper. Louis scanned the gifts while he waited for Mobley to finish flirting. A bottle of Leopold's Gin with a card that read: Gin makes you sin. Three cans of John Frieda hair mousse duct-taped together. A bundle of cigars. And a twelve-pack of animal print condoms.

Louis had known Mobley a few years now. Knew he was a publicity hound, an office iron-pumper, a ladies' man, a closeted lounge pianist. But probably most important, he was a competent sheriff who used his charm and good looks to mask his lack of good judgment and investigative skills.

Louis glanced around the bar. Half the Lee County cops — and more than handful of city cops — were here. No matter what Mobley was, his men liked him. And that was important.

Mobley's voice broke his thoughts. "Sit down, Kincaid."

Louis slid into the booth. Mobley grabbed a bottle of Jack Daniels and poured himself another shot.

"You want a drink?" Mobley asked.

"Sure."

Mobley tried to signal the bartender, and when he was ignored he searched the cluttered table for an empty glass. He
found a used shot glass beneath a crumple of gold paper and
filled it for Louis.

Louis let it sit in front of him.

"So what did you want to talk to me about that was so important you're interrupting my birthday party?"

"You told me to meet you here," Louis said. "You never said
you'd be at a party."

"Fuck it," Mobley said. "Talk to me."

Louis glanced down at the whiskey and decided to drink it.
His throat was still burning when he spoke.

"I'm here to ask you for a job," Louis said.

Mobley's brow shot up and his eyes took a moment to focus.
The bar was noisier than hell but suddenly it seemed as if there
was no one here but the two of them.

"I want back inside," Louis said. "I want to wear a badge
again."

Mobley continued to stare at him, but as understanding sank
in, his lips tipped up in a small smile.

"And I didn't think this day could get any better," he said.

Someone slapped Mobley on the back of the head, mumbled
something about the sheriff getting lucky tonight and wandered
away. Mobley paid him no attention, his gaze still on Louis.

"You're too old," Mobley said.

"I'm twenty-nine."

"You look thirty-five easy."

"It's seasoning."

"You're too controversial, too well known as a PI," Mobley
said. "I don't need any deputies who get their names in the papers."

"You mean deputies who get their names in the papers more than you do."

"See, that attitude is exactly what I'm talking about," Mobley said. "You've been rogue too long. You've forgotten what it's all about, lost respect for things like protocol and rank."

Louis leaned over the table. "Listen to me," he said. "I graduated pre-law from Michigan. I trained in one of the best police academies in the country and graduated third in my class. I've been shot at, stabbed and nearly hanged and have worked with some of the best investigators in this state and in Michigan on half a dozen cold cases. With all due respect, you have no idea what kind of cop I was or what kind I will be. Sir."

Mobley's dimmed expression never changed. For a few moments, the bar was a cacophony of noises — clinking glasses, deep-throated laughter and the pounding music of Guns N' Roses's *Welcome to the Jungle*.

"No," Mobley said, turning back to his drink. "Go ask Chief Horton for a job. He seems to like you."

"The city is on a hiring freeze," Louis said. "You're not. I saw the notice two days in the newspaper."

"We're hiring deputies only," Mobley said.

"I don't care where I start."

"I said no."

Louis sat back, staring at the empty shot glass in front of him. He hadn't wanted to make the argument he was about to make — it seemed desperate and self-serving to use the fact that he was black to pry an opening in the tightly shut door. But truth was, his color was exactly what Mobley needed right now.

"I also read something else in the newspaper," Louis said. "Your department is facing seventeen counts of employment discrimination. I hear the justice department is coming down to review your hiring and promotion files."

Mobley shoved his glass aside and leaned into Louis. "Those charges are bullshit. I don't have a bigoted bone in my body. Everyone knows that."

"I guess you can tell that to the DOJ when they get here," Louis said. "And trust me, once they get a hold of you they never let go."

Mobley was quiet, grinding his jaw.

"Did you know," Louis continued, "that there are some police departments in the south that are still under DOJ hiring quotas from the 1960s?"

"You've managed to sink lower than I thought possible," Mobley said. "Threatening me with discrimination. Get out of my bar."

Louis didn't move, instead ordering two beers to give Mobley time to simmer down. After the waitress delivered the beers and the sheriff had taken a long pull from his bottle, Louis went on.

"Listen, sheriff," he said. "I don't like affirmative action either, though I know that there are some companies that still need it forced down their throats. But I never took advantage. I didn't even put my race down on my college application."

"So what's your point?"

"My point is, you need some brown faces in your department and you've got one right in front of you asking you for a job."

Mobley shook his head. "You don't get it, Kincaid," he said. "We've gone out of our way to find qualified minorities. I'm not stupid. I know I can't police this community with nothing but white men, but I'm telling you the quality of human being I need just isn't out there."

"Maybe you haven't looked in the right places."

"I have a damn good recruitment division," Mobley said. "And we're going to solve this so-called race problem. I don't need you and all the dead bodies you seem attract."

Louis looked away, hand around the beer bottle. He knew Mobley wouldn't make it easy, knew he'd have to grovel some, but he had thought he could talk him into it. Though he still had his detractors, his reputation as a PI in southwest Florida was impressive and he knew he might be able to take that to a place like Miami or Orlando. But damn it, he wanted to stay here, in Fort Myers, on Captiva, in his little gray cottage. Near the water. Near the handful of people he had let into his life.

"Lance," someone called, "You got a call at the bar."

"Tell them I'm in the shitter."

"It's Undersheriff Portman. Better take it."

Mobley mumbled something and looked to Louis as he started a long slide out of the booth. "I got to take this," he said. "Don't be here where I get back."

Louis watched Mobley stagger toward the bar where he leaned on his elbows and picked up the phone. Louis drew a breath and put a five on the table.

Half-way to the door, he stopped and took another look around O'Sullivan's. It was one level above a dive with its sputtering neon and cracked leather booths. He had never found a place like this when he was wearing a badge. Back in Ann Arbor, flush with a criminology degree and a rookie's idealism, he had decided he was too smart, too good to be part of the gritty off-duty lifestyle of a cop. And in Mississippi, the only tavern in town had been decorated with a confederate flag.

Outside, the August air was still and scorched-smelling, baking the buildings and sidewalk like they were rocks in a kiln. Louis headed toward his Mustang.

"Kincaid."

Louis turned to see Mobley standing in the doorway of the bar. His hair was the color of hay, his skin as bronzed as a lifeguard. A cigarette hung limply from the side of his mouth.

"You really serious about wearing a uniform again?" Mobley asked.

"I told you I was."

"Okay, I'll give you a shot."

"A shot?"

Mobley tried to take the cigarette from his mouth but the paper stuck to his dry lip and he had to peel it off. It took him a moment to refocus on Louis.

"I got this situation going on I'm going to deputize you for."

"Deputize me?" Louis asked. "Is that even still legal?"

"Yeah, kind of," Mobley said. "Anyway, doesn't really matter. I can do what I want."

"Right."

"You'll get a temporary badge and ID card," Mobley said, "but no uniform. You'll wear street clothes. Jacket and tie."

In ninety-nine-degree heat. Mobley was screwing with him but that was okay. He had a jacket. Somewhere. In his trunk maybe, from that last case he had worked over in Palm Beach.

"So, consider this a test, Kincaid," Mobley said. "You pass it — and only I decide if you do — and I'll get you in front of my hiring board with a five-star recommendation."

"You got a deal," Louis said. "When do I start?"

"I'll get you your credentials tomorrow, but you can start right now."

Louis squinted up at the sun. It was already three. He looked back at Mobley.

"Okay, what's the job?"

"I want you to go pick up a dead cat."

CHAPTER TWO

I t wasn't just any cat.

This one weighed about a hundred and thirty pounds and had claws that could rip a man to shreds.

The panther was lying on its side, motionless, on the baking concrete of the pool deck. Louis stood about ten feet away, sweat dripping down his face, muscles tensed. He moved closer. Close enough to see the cat's big pink tongue hanging from its mouth.

"Is it dead? It's dead, right?"

He glanced back at the old woman standing at the open sliding glass door. She was holding a small poodle whose curly white hair and anxious eyes matched her own. The damn dog had barked non-stop from the moment Louis set foot on the patio but at least for the moment it was just shaking, like it was having a seizure.

"Yes, ma'am, I think it's dead."

The pool pump kicked on with a loud groan and gushing noise.

The poodle went into a barking frenzy. Louis looked back at the woman who was trying hard to keep it from jumping out of her arms. When he looked back at the big cat it still wasn't moving.

No, it wasn't dead. Its chest was moving, just barely.

"Ma'am," he called back over his shoulder. "I think you'd better take your dog inside."

"What?"

"Please go inside the house."

He waited until he heard the sliding door close. The barking was muted now at least. He crept closer to the cat and squatted down.

It was about seven feet long from nose to tail's end with a tawny brown coat that was white on the belly and tipped in black on the tail and ears. Its yellow eyes were open but unfocused and its mouth hung open, showing its tongue and large teeth.

Louis had never seen one alive before, just pictures in magazines and those black silhouettes on the road signs cautioning people to drive slower. But he knew it was a Florida panther. He knew, too, that there weren't many left in the wild. And he knew that this one was dying.

He craned his neck, trying to get a better look at the big cat but he couldn't see any wounds or any blood. The only thing that seemed off was that the animal looked too thin. Louis could see the gentle rippling of its ribs as it labored to breathe.

Louis jerked the radio from the back pocket of his chinos and keyed the special frequency Mobley had assigned him.

"Kincaid to Lee County base."

A pause. "Identify again?"

"Kincaid. Louis Kincaid."

Another pause. "Who is this?"

"Kincaid. I'm on temporary assignment for Sheriff Mobley and–"

"One moment."

The radio went silent. Louis wiped his sweating face and looked down at the panther. He couldn't see the chest moving anymore. He inched closer and gently nudged a back paw with his shoe. The leg moved and Louis jerked back.

The radio squawked to life. "Okay, Mr. Kincaid. What's your business?" It was a woman dispatcher. She sounded young, with the sweet calming tone of a kindergarten teacher.

"I need to speak to the sheriff ASAP."

"He's unavailable."

Louis glanced at his watch. It was past four. Mobley was probably still at O'Sullivan's laughing his ass off.

"Miss, I could use some help here," Louis said. "I've got a Florida panther here on someone's patio and —"

"Panther?"

"Yeah, it's —"

"You're sure it's a panther?"

"Yeah, I'm sure."

"Does it match the BOLO description?"

BOLO? What the hell?

"Read me the BOLO, please," Louis said.

The dispatcher read the be-on-the-lookout alert put out by the Fish and Game Conservation Commission. As far as Louis could tell the description matched the panther, right down to the bulky radio collar it was wearing.

"Is it dead?" the dispatcher asked.

"Not yet."

And that was what was going to help Louis pass Mobley's damn test. He knew Mobley didn't care about a dead cat. A dead panther found in the wild wasn't news. The sad fact was that the cats were routinely killed by cars. But a rescued live panther found on an old lady's patio in Lehigh Acres was another story. A story that the TV cameras — and Lance Mobley — wouldn't be able to resist.

"I need to contact the Fish and Wildlife people," Louis said. "Can you patch me through to someone, please?"

"I can notify them for you."

"I'd like to speak to them myself," Louis said.

"One moment, Mr. Kincaid."

A minute later a man came on the line and Louis told him about the panther on the patio. The man asked no questions, only for directions to Elsie Kaufman's house. He asked Louis to stay until a ranger arrived.

Louis thanked the dispatcher and clicked off. He looked back at the sliding glass door. Elsie Kaufman was still standing there clutching her poodle, staring out at him. He looked up at big clock-sized thermometer on the house. It read ninety-five.

Fuck this.

He tore off his tie and blazer and tossed them toward a lounge chair, his eyes still locked on the panther.

He crept back to the animal and squatted down, about four feet away. Maybe he was too close but he didn't think so. The cat's eyes opened for second then closed again.

"Hang on, cat," he said.

CHAPTER THREE

It was almost five but the slanting sun was still beating down on the patio full-force. Louis had retreated to the overhang near the sliding glass door with the glass of lemonade Elsie Kaufman had given him. The panther had not moved but Louis could see from his vantage point it was still breathing.

He heard the click of a gate latch and looked up. Two men in khaki shorts and white short-sleeved shirts had come onto the patio. As they came closer, Louis saw the large patches on their shirts – FWC for Florida Wildlife Commission — and the radios on their belts.

"You the officer who called us?" one guy said, coming to Louis. The other guy headed straight to the panther.

"Yeah," Louis said.

"Any idea how long it's been here?"

"I've been here about forty-five minutes."

"What about before that?"

"No idea. Is it important?"

"Yes."

The guy joined the other ranger. Louis heard the gate open again and a third man came onto the patio. He was stocky but shorter than the others, dressed the same except for a FWC ball cap and big aviator sunglasses. He was carrying a black duffel and went quickly to the panther without a look at Louis.

"You want the crate, doc?" one man asked the small guy.

"Let me get a look first."

The two taller rangers took a couple steps back to give the smaller man room to kneel by the panther. Louis came up behind them and watched as the small guy took a syringe and carefully injected something into the cat's fleshy nape. The animal gave a slight jerk then laid its big head back on the concrete.

The guy in the ball cap — Louis figured he was a vet — waited a few seconds then began to examine the animal, running his palms over its fur, moving from the neck and down over the ribs. He then went on to test each limb, gently manipulating first the front legs then the back ones.

"I think the back right leg is fractured," he said. "Better go get a board, Jeff."

When the vet glanced his way, Louis caught a glimpse of his face beneath the ball cap brim. It was smooth, brown-skinned and boyish. The mirrored aviator glasses glinted in the slanting sun as the vet stared up at him.

Louis heard the scrape of the sliding glass door and turned to see Elsie Kaufman peering out, the trembling poodle still in her arms.

"Angel has to poop," she said.

"You can't let your dog out, ma'am," Louis said, going to the door. "You'll have to take her to the front yard."

"She never goes out in the front." She pointed to a spot of yellow grass in the corner of the yard. "She'll only poop over there."

"Ma'am —"

"And she didn't poop this morning."

"Your dog only uses the backyard?"

She nodded. "Yes, she doesn't like to go out on the street because the kids on their bikes scare her."

"What time did you let her out here this morning?"

"At seven. I always let her out right after Willard does the weather."

"You told me that you noticed the panther out here only because your dog started barking. Did she bark in the morning when you let her out?"

Elsie Kaufman shook her head. "She piddled and came right back in. I let her out again right before three. That's when I heard her go crazy barking. I came out here and when I saw that animal I brought Angel right back in and called nine-one-one."

"You're sure it was three?"

"Yup. *General Hospital* was just coming on. I missed the first ten minutes, damn it." She craned her neck to look beyond Louis. "How long does it take to pick up a dead cat anyway? If Angel poops on my carpet one of you is going to come in and clean it up, you hear?"

She closed the door. When Louis looked back at the rangers, the two large ones were carefully strapping the panther onto a board.

The vet zipped up the duffel and came up to Louis. "Thanks for calling us."

It was only then that Louis realized the vet was a woman. She had taken off her ball cap to wipe her face and her ponytail had come loose, hanging over her shoulder. When she took off her sunglasses he got a good look at her eyes — large, soft brown and long-lashed.

"No problem," Louis said. "Is the panther okay?"

"He's really dehydrated. That's probably why he wandered into this yard, to drink from the pool." She shook her head slowly. "But how in the hell he got here with that leg is beyond me."

Louis had been wondering the exact same thing. Elsie Kaufman's house was in a dense cookie-cutter subdivision called Lehigh Acres, a good thirty miles inland from the gulf and about twenty miles from the eastern city limits of Fort Myers.

On his travels from the west coast over to Miami, Louis had seen the big road signs — WARNING PANTHER HABITAT. But the signs were out on Alligator Alley, the interstate that cut across the Everglades, and that was a good ways south of here.

"I thought panthers lived down in the Everglades," Louis said.

"Most do. But this one's an Oka cat."

"A what cat?"

"Oka cat. There's a small isolated population that lives up here in the Okaloacoochee Slough. That's in the Corkscrew Swamp Sanctuary only about twenty miles due east of here. Bruce is an Oka cat."

"Bruce?"

She had been watching the other FWC rangers and when she turned back to Louis a small smile tipped her lips. "I name all my panthers."

"Your panthers?"

"Yeah. They're my panthers. All thirty-two of them." Her smile faded as her eyes drifted back to the cat lying on the board. She looked back at Louis. "I don't want to lose another one. I better get him back to the hospital."

She started to leave.

"Oh, by the way," Louis said, "I found out it the — Bruce — showed up here on the patio between seven this morning and three this afternoon."

She nodded. "That's helpful. His radio collar malfunctioned so we didn't even know he was in trouble."

"So why'd you put out a BOLO for him."

She took off her sunglasses. "BOLO?"

"Yeah, the notice you guys put out to law enforcement agencies that you had a missing panther."

"We didn't send out a notice for Bruce. The panther we're looking for is a female. Her name is Grace. And she's still missing."

"Doesn't she have a radio collar, too?"

"Yeah, but it's not sending out a signal."

The sound of the gate closing made her look away. "I have to go," she said. "I need to get Bruce to the hospital." She started away but then turned back.

"Thanks for staying with him," she said.

"No problem," he said. "I have a cat myself."

She gave him an odd stare then walked away, disappearing through the gate.

Louis looked back at the sliding glass door. The old lady with the poodle slid it open a crack.

"Can we come out now?" she asked.

"Yeah, they're gone."

He looked up at the reddening western sky. It had to be past six. Maybe if he hurried he could still catch Mobley at O'Sullivan's.

His blazer and tie...

He turned to the lounge chair to grab them but froze. The blazer was floating out in the middle of the pool.

He glanced around but there was no leaf scoop, nothing he could use to retrieve the blazer. For a second he thought of jumping in and getting the damn thing.

To hell with it.

The panther was alive. This joke of a case was over. And so were his chances of getting back in uniform.

He picked up the tie, tossed it in the pool and left.

CHAPTER FOUR

A soft touch on his face woke him as usual. Louis pushed her away but she persisted. Finally, with a sigh, he opened his eyes.

"Come on, give a guy a break," he said.

Another caress on his cheek.

He looked down at the black cat sitting next to him. It reached out a paw and tapped his cheek again then sat staring at him until he finally pushed back the damp sheets and got up.

"Okay, okay."

The cat followed him through the bedroom and living room and out onto the porch. He held the screen door open and the cat slipped out. It stood for a moment in the sandy yard then trotted off into the sea oats.

Louis bent to retrieve the copies of the *Fort Myers News Press* and the *Island Reporter*. He stood on the porch yawning, squinting into the shimmering gulf. He went back inside his cottage, pausing to bang a fist on the rattling wall-unit air conditioner. It wheezed and groaned but the air didn't get any cooler. He switched it off. Blessed quiet filled the small cottage. The only sound was the whisper of the surf and the slap of his bare feet on the terrazzo as he headed to the kitchen.

As he waited for the Mr. Coffee to drip, he scanned the front page of the *News Press* but there was nothing of interest. Not that he expected the news about the panther to make the papers. He had dutifully reported his call on Elsie Kaufman yesterday but he had gotten back to the sheriff's office too late to talk to Mobley. It would wait until later when he went in to get his temporary credentials.

After he stirred sugar into his coffee and took a quick gulp, he shook a bag of Tender Vittles into a bowl and refilled the water dish. When he went back onto the porch, Issy was waiting for him. He held open the door and the cat came in.

"That was quick. Too hot for you, too, huh?"

The cat went to its food, scarfed it down and began to lap up water. Louis watched her, noticing for the first time that she looked thinner than usual. Not that he ever paid that close attention. Issy had been a shadowy presence in his cottage for five years now. He had taken the cat in after she was accidently abandoned by a woman he had been involved with in Michigan.

He had never liked cats much, but now, as he looked down at Issy he had to admit he had come to like having her around. It wasn't like have a dog or something. All he had to do is let her out and in, toss some food in her bowl and pick up the dead lizards she left on his bed. She made no real demands on him. She was the perfect companion.

He made a mental note to call the vet and picked up his coffee, heading to the bedroom.

The phone rang, pulling him back to the kitchen counter.

"Hello?" he said, sliding onto a stool.

"Mr. Kincaid? Louis Kincaid?"

"You found me. Who's this?"

"Katy Letka."

"I'm sorry...who?"

"Katy Letka. I'm the FWC vet who came to get the panther yesterday."

"Oh, yeah. Right."

"Listen, I know it's early but this is important. I called the sheriff's department to find you and they said you're really a private investigator."

"Yeah, I'm on a special assignment with the sheriff's department for now."

"Well, I need some special help."

Louis waited, stirring one more sugar into his coffee, wondering what had driven Katy Letka to call him — a cheating boyfriend, a deadbeat dad?

"This is about Grace," she said. "We found her collar early this morning. It had been cut off."

"Don't you have investigators?"

"We used to have a guy but he got canned in staff cutbacks and he wasn't very good anyway," she said. "And this is not the usual thing we investigate. This isn't normal. Something's wrong. I think Grace has been abducted. Will you help me?"

"Abducted? Who would abduct a wild animal?"

"I don't know. That's the problem. I don't know where to go with this."

Louis paced slowly around the kitchen. He wanted to help. He had already been assigned to the case, even though Mobley had probably done it as a joke. But it wasn't a joke to Katy Letka.

"All right," he said. "Where do we start?"

"I'll show you where we found the collar. There's a place in Immokalee where we can meet up — Juan's."

"I know it."

Juan's Place was a red and white cinderblock bodega favored by the migrant fruit pickers who made up a good portion of Immokalee's population.

Louis pulled into the dusty lot and spotted the van with the FWC emblem among the rusty pickups. When he swung his white Mustang alongside, Katy Letka got out of the van. She was wearing the ball cap, a long-sleeved white shirt and khaki pants, the kind with Velcro pockets and zippers at the knees that could convert the pants into shorts with the flick of a wrist.

Even in his t-shirt and jeans, Louis was sweating by the time he approached the door of her van.

"I took the liberty," she said, holding out a tiny Styrofoam cup.

"Thanks," Louis said, staring down into the ink-black coffee. "Any sugar?"

With a rip of a Velcro pocket she produced three packs and a plastic stir.

As Louis sipped his coffee his eyes locked on the huge vehicle sitting on the other side of the FWC van. With its monstrous gnarled tires and stripped-down frame it looked like an ATV on steroids. There was a large empty cage in the back. One of the two FWC guys who had showed up to rescue the panther yesterday was loading bottled water into a cooler. Like Katy Letka, he was dressed in long pants and a long-sleeved shirt.

"So where are we going exactly?" Louis asked.

"About ten miles southeast of here," Katy said. "In the middle of the Okaloacoochee Slough." She eyed Louis's '65 Mustang convertible. "Your car won't make it. You'll have to ride out with us in the swamp buggy."

Louis downed the coffee and followed her to the back of the ATV.

"You might want to put this on over your t-shirt," she said, holding out a wad of clothing.

"Why?"

"Where we're headed the forecast is ninety-eight degrees with a hundred-percent chance of insects."

Louis shook out the wrinkled long-sleeved shirt with a FWC emblem on the pocket, slipped it on and climbed into the back seat.

The swamp buggy came alive with a roar. The guy behind the wheel turned and stuck out a hand. "I'm Daryl," he said with a smile. "Better buckle up."

About ten minutes outside town, they left the blacktop road for a gravel turnoff and were soon rumbling through heavy brush. Then the gravel disappeared leaving only two ruts in the deep yellow grass. Squat palmetto palms swiped at the sides of the swamp buggy. It was so jarring Louis had to grit his teeth. Talk was impossible, so he let his mind wander as his eyes moved over the jungle-like terrain.

He had been in a place like this once before, a desolate spot called Starvation Prairie, where he and Joe had hunted a child kidnapper. It had been the case that had brought them together. She was a Miami homicide detective, he was a PI. They had ended up lovers.

Joe...

It had been easy when she was still in Miami, just three hours away from him across Alligator Alley. But now she was in Michigan and there was more than just miles between them.

The swamp buggy jerked to a stop. The engine roar was replaced by a silence so thick he could feel the pressure in his eardrums.

Then came the drone of insects.

He felt a tug on his arm. Katy was holding out a blue plastic bottle. "Here," she said.

Louis took the bottle. "Avon Skin So Soft?"

"Best mosquito repellent on earth."

He sprayed his face and neck and jumped down from the buggy. The ground was spongy with pine needles, the air soupy with smells like things were dying all around him. He fell into step behind Daryl and Katy as they pushed through the brush.

Louis spotted a strip of yellow tape tied around a tree. Katy stopped at the tree and held out a large plastic bag to Louis.

"This is where we found her collar," she said.

Louis took the plastic bag. The collar inside looked just like the one Bruce wore, except it had been cut.

He fingered the radio unit through the plastic. "Okay, I don't know much about panthers," he said. "Let's start at the beginning. How did you know that it...Grace was missing?"

"Most our panthers are collared. Every two days, our plane goes up to give us readings on their radios."

She glanced up at the heat-hazed sky and wiped her brow.

"Normally, a female panther's territory is about seventy-miles and Grace had stopped moving," she said. "I wasn't worried because I thought she might be denning."

"Denning?" Louis asked.

"When they're getting ready to have kittens, they reduce their range," Katy said. "But then the radio signal went dead."

"That's why you put out the BOLO?"

She nodded. "Sometimes the radios malfunction. We wanted the rural deputies to keep an eye out for her just in case she was hit by a car. This morning, while we were searching her last co-ordinates, we found her collar. When we saw it was cut off I knew something was wrong."

"Poachers?" Louis asked.

"There's only two poaching cases we know of," she said. "One was a hunter who said he shot the panther because he was threatened. Which is ridiculous because panthers are shy. They stay away from hu-mans."

"And the other guy?"

"Some rich asshole who got drunk with his friends and de-cided he wanted a stuffed panther head mounted on his wall. One of his buddies turned him in. He's doing five to ten up in Raiford."

Louis peered at the collar through the plastic, fingering the cut in the heavy leather. It had been sawed off with a large blade.

"Did you find any blood here?" he asked.

"Blood?" Katy asked.

"From Grace."

She shook her head. "We looked, in about a twenty-yard ra-dius but we didn't see anything to indicate she was hurt."

"Then she had to have been tranquilized."

Katy just nodded, still looking around the brush like she had maybe missed something.

"He wanted her alive," Louis said. "What would someone do with a live panther?"

She looked up at him. "I don't know."

Louis walked away, eyes to the ground. Every crime scene was the same — the perp always left something of himself and always took something away. It could be a discarded cigarette butt or dirt picked up in the tread of a sneaker.

In this jungle, evidence was going to be hard to find. But not impossible. Lee County's CSI team was one of the state's best. It was just a matter of getting Mobley to cough up the money and manpower for a missing cat.

The squawk of a radio drew Louis's attention back to Katy. He was too far away to hear the conversation. When Katy signed off, she waved him over.

"I got the lab work on Bruce," she said. "They found acepromazine in his system."

"What's that?"

"It's a tranquilizer," she said.

"I thought you tranquilized him on the patio?"

"No, acepromazine is a damn horse tranquilizer," she said. "The injection site was his chest. He was darted."

Louis was confused. "So how'd he break his leg?"

She didn't seem to hear him. She was staring at something in the distance, her jaw clenched.

"Katy? How'd he break his leg?"

"He must have climbed a tree," she said, pointing to a towering tree. "They do that when they feel threatened. He was darted and fell."

Louis shaded his eyes to look up at the spindly cypress tree. "How long do they stay out?"

"Half hour, maybe forty-five minutes."

"Plenty of time for someone to load a panther into a cage in a truck and get away someplace isolated."

Katy nodded.

"Grace went missing first, right?" Louis asked.

"Yeah."

"Maybe he wanted two," Louis said. "A male and a female."

He wiped the sweat from his face and looked back at Katy.

"How many panthers are left in the wild?" he asked.

"Maybe thirty," Katy said. She hesitated. "We're losing them fast."

"Well, maybe someone's building an ark," Louis said.

CHAPTER FIVE

All the way across town, he heard sirens. As he pulled into the parking lot of the Lee County Administration Building, he remembered something a female cop had once told him. The sudden swell of multiple sirens was like a baby's cries — experience told you just how serious it was.

A couple sirens, combined with an ambulance or two, probably indicated a traffic accident on a major road. Sheriff's cars streaming in one direction was likely a backup situation for an officer in trouble. Cruisers from every agency whizzing through every red light meant something big was going down.

And that's what was happening now.

He parked his Mustang in the visitor's lot and picked up the envelope Katy had given him. He knew he would need ammunition to convince Mobley this panther thing was worth his department's time, and Katy had obligated with some stunning photographs.

"Maybe it will make it real for him," she had said.

Louis wasn't sure anything could warm Lance Mobley's heart besides a double shot of Jack Daniels but it was worth a try.

Mobley's office was down the first corridor, the double glass doors marked by the five-star county seal and Mobley's name in large gold letters.

The secretary was on the phone, but her eyes darted up to Louis as he came in. Louis didn't know her but she bore a stark resemblance to all the secretaries Louis had seen at this desk before her. A toned, sun-streaked blonde who wore a bright print blouse and a Slinky-like bunch of silver bracelets.

She finally hung up the phone and drawing a weary breath looked again to Louis. "Yes?"

"I'm Louis Kincaid. The sheriff is expecting me."

He could see from the blank expression on her face she couldn't place his name.

"The panther? I'm working with the Fish and Game —"

"Oh, yeah. I'm sorry. Things are a little chaotic right now."

"What's going on? I heard the sirens."

"Armed robbery in Estero," she said. "Three wounded officers, one suspect was shot at the scene, two others fled in a green Monte Carlo. The entire county is in pursuit."

Louis looked toward Mobley's open office door. The high-backed leather chair was empty. Mobley would be tied up all day with a situation like this, especially if it was his department that eventually took down the robbers.

Which meant a missing panther was low priority for Mobley right now. Still, Louis had a crime scene waiting to be processed and each additional day left it open to contamination.

He looked back at the secretary. "Should I wait —"

The door behind him banged open and Mobley came in. His green and white uniform was dark with sweat. His eyes shot briefly to Louis then he walked to the secretary's desk, snatched his messages from her outstretched hand and moved quickly into his office. He left the door open and Louis took it as a gesture to follow.

The first thing Mobley did was reach over to turn up the volume on the police radio. Red lights zipped back and forth on five channels. To anyone else, the radio traffic would have sounded like excited gibberish but Louis understood every word. The wounded officers had already been released from the hospital, Collier County S.O. had joined the pursuit, and the fleeing suspects had caused a traffic accident on Tamiami but had managed to drive on, dragging a sparking fender behind them.

Mobley glanced at Louis. "I don't have time right now for you and your dead cat," he said.

"He wasn't dead," Louis said. "He was —"

Mobley held up a hand to silence him as he leaned toward the radio. The suspects had entered I-75, heading south at a high speed. One of Mobley's deputies radioed in for permission to continue the pursuit in what was suddenly far more dangerous conditions — a crowded freeway. The deputy sounded young, his strained voice nearly drowned out by the screaming siren in the background. A superior officer, also in the chase, gave him the okay to continue.

Mobley hadn't sat down, hadn't moved from his spot behind his desk. He reminded Louis of how Susan Outlaw looked a few years ago when she was waiting for news on her son Ben after he'd been kidnapped. It was a combination of emotions: fear for those you cared about and helplessness because you couldn't be out there to help.

For the next five or six minutes, they listened to the anxious chatter of officers and wailing sirens. Then suddenly it was over, the young deputy's voice dominating the others as he announced that the Monte Carlo had clipped a semi, went airborne and flipped until it was nearly cut in half by a tree. With a small break in his voice he ended his transmission with, "both suspects appear to be DOA."

Mobley keyed the radio and asked for the exact location of the roll-over. He was told the pursuit had ended two miles north of the Collier County line, in Lee County.

Mobley's turf. Mobley's headlines.

Mobley turned the radio down, walked to the open door and told the secretary to schedule a press conference in an hour. He came back to his desk and dropped into his chair.

"You got about thirty seconds before I get slammed," he said.

"The panther wasn't dead," Louis said. "It was illegally darted, fell from a tree and went looking for water."

"Sounds like hunter trying to poach a trophy."

"It's not a poaching incident," Louis said. "The wounded panther was not the same cat Fish and Game put the BOLO out on. That was a female cat named Grace. And we know for a fact that she's been abducted, probably by the same person who tried to take Bruce."

"Bruce?"

"The male cat in Lehigh Acres."

Mobley's eyes came up to Louis's face, flickering with disbelief. "I'm about to coordinate the processing of an armed robbery scene with multiple fatalities and you're giving me some fairy tale about kidnapped cats?"

"I can appreciate your position," Louis said. "But there's only a handful of panthers left out there. Fish and Game monitors them very closely. It's a federal crime to even mess with the cats."

"But not our crime, Kincaid."

"You're wrong," Louis said. "It is our crime. You gave it to me."

Mobley smiled. "You thought I was serious?"

Louis felt sucker-punched. He had thought Mobley was serious, at least as far as seeing just how much shit Louis would take to wear a badge again.

"Yeah," Louis said. "I thought you were being straight with me because I thought you were a man of your word. Even when you were drunk."

Mobley's smile vanished and his face flushed with color as he glared at Louis. The phone started ringing but Mobley made no move to answer it. Finally, the secretary intercepted it and the office was quiet again. Mobley was still staring at him so Louis decided he'd simply keep arguing.

"I don't think the cat-napper is a trophy hunter," Louis said. "I think he wanted to mate the male and female panthers. But the male, Bruce, got away from him."

"Okay, I'll bite,' Mobley said. "Why would a guy want a litter of panther kitties?"

"Maybe he wants his own family of cats," Louis said, thinking of the strange people who lived in the Everglades in shanties and tents. "Maybe he's trying to help stave off extinction. I don't know. But I do know that if I'm right about him wanting to mate two panthers, he will come back for another male. And when he does, someone could get hurt."

Mobley's phone started ringing and again he ignored it. His gaze dropped to Louis's hand. "What do you have in that envelope?" he asked.

Louis opened the envelope and dumped the photographs Katy had given him on the desk. Most were shots of Bruce and Grace, obviously taken with telephoto lenses, but with an artist's eye for the beauty of the lithe animals.

The last four pictures were of Bruce lying half-dead on the Lehigh Acres patio, Bruce with his leg splinted, a close-up shot of Grace's severed collar and last, a picture of Katy holding a spotted panther kitten, back-dropped by the green foliage of the Everglades.

"Who's this?" Mobley asked.

"The Fish and Game officer in charge of the panthers."

Mobley sifted through the photos. The phone started up again, this time followed a second ringing on the other line.

Voices echoed from down the hall. Louis knew his time was running out.

"Sheriff," Louis said. "Everyone loves a good animal rescue story. Think of the great PR you'll get when we find Grace."

"It's only great PR if you find the thing alive, Kincaid." Mobley tossed the photos down and stood up. "What do you need?"

"A CSI team in the Everglades as soon as possible," Louis said. "I could use some techs who specialize in tire and animal tracks."

Mobley gave him a withering look. "What else?"

"I want to talk to people who've been arrested for animal abuse or poaching in the Everglades," Louis said. "So, I'll need access to your criminal database."

"I'll have Ginger arrange authorization."

"I'll also need a four-wheel drive vehicle."

A clamor of voices rose in the outer office. Louis glanced over his shoulder to see a huddle of men in suits and sweaty uniformed officers waiting to see Mobley. Behind them, he spotted a TV cameraman.

When he turned back, Mobley was holding out a small leather wallet.

"You'll need this, too," Mobley said.

Louis took the wallet and opened it. On one side was a gold deputy's badge with the Lee County Sheriff's seal. On the other, where the official ID would go, was a white card with the sheriff's office logo embossed across the top. Underneath, it read: The courtesies and law enforcement authority of this office have been temporarily extended to Louis Kincaid. It was signed by Sheriff Lance S. Mobley.

"I do keep my word, Kincaid," Mobley said. "Now go find that damn cat. Alive."

CHAPTER SIX

After leaving Mobley, Louis felt the need to burn off the extra adrenalin of the day, so he stopped by Gold's Gym and did a quick hour in the weight room.

That wasn't enough so he swung by Fowler Firearms and killed another hour target shooting with his Glock. It was Friday — Ladies Shoot Free! — and the place was packed with women laying waste to paper Zombies with pink Sig Skeeters.

He didn't mind being the lone male. He had been avoiding going to the Lee County Gun Range lately because he didn't want to run into any cops who might get curious about why he was sharpening his shooting skills. Not yet at least. Not until he was sure he had a permanent deputy badge on his chest.

Eventually he'd have to break down and go to the Lee County range. He was going to have to do the tactical training course, test his accuracy shooting at the computer-controlled moving targets that mimicked what a cop might encounter on the street. It was one thing to shoot at static paper silhouettes. It was something else entirely to make split-second decisions on random moving targets.

He hadn't done tactical training since the academy. He knew he was rusty. Just like he knew his body had gone a little soft and his credit needed cleaning up. It didn't matter. He was willing to do whatever it took to get back inside.

It was past five by the time he got home. He fed Issy, peeled off his sticky clothes and took a long cool shower to get rid of the film of sweat and Avon Skin So Soft.

A breeze was blowing in from the Gulf when he emerged from the bathroom, towel around his waist, so he didn't bother to turn on the air conditioning. When he went to the refrigerator to get a Heineken he caught the faint scent of gun-powder. His Glock was lying on the kitchen counter where he had left it.

He had planned to go through his mail and phone messages but all that would have to wait.

He pulled what he needed from a kitchen drawer, tucked the towel tighter around his waist and sat down on a stool at the counter.

The ritual was always the same. And there was something oddly calming about it.

He grasped the Glock and dropped out the magazine, setting it aside. Next, he made sure the chamber was clear. He'd never accidently fired a weapon while cleaning it but he once knew a cop who did. The stray bullet had killed him.

Dismantling the Glock had taken him some time to master. It wasn't like the old model 10 revolvers or the simply assembled shotguns he'd used as a rookie. The Glock was a little like one of those wooden block puzzles where each movement had to be done in the correct order to open it up.

First, he pulled the trigger until it clicked back into place. With a claw-like grip on the top of the gun, he pressed a tab and the slide came off.

He squirted a little Hoppes oil into the three pieces — the spring, the slide and the barrel — then wiped each dry with a piece of an old t-shirt. The Glock's frame was polymer but he always took the time to blow away the gun powder residue from the crevices.

As he reassembled the Glock, he thought of Bud. He was his firearms instructor back at the academy, a small soft-spoken bald man whose quiet reverence for guns had earned him the name of the Buddha. He could still hear Bud's words.

Take care of it and it will take care of you. For those of you who ride alone it is the only partner you'll have.

Louis reassembled the Glock, slid it back in its holster and set it on the counter. The phone messages were still waiting. He hit the rewind button.

"Hey Rocky, how the hell are you?"

It was Mel. He had met the ex-Miami detective on a case here on Captiva Island years ago and they had forged one of those old-marriage bonds that withstood the benign neglect that colored most male friendships.

"Look, we need to get together," Mel went on. "Yuba and I are going over to the Roadhouse Saturday night to see Lou Colombo. We want you to come with us and don't give me that shit that you have plans because I know you never do. Call me."

Louis took a long draw from the Heineken. He hadn't seen Mel since that case they worked together over in Palm Beach last Christmas. Yuba was a lovely East Indian bartender who had followed Mel back to Fort Myers. Mel never admitted it, but Louis knew they were in love.

That Palm Beach case had been seven months ago. Where had the time gone?

The next voice was a male and at first Louis didn't recognize it.

"Hey, Louis, are you there? Pick up, dude! I guess you're not home. But you're never home."

It was Ben, the boy whom Louis had befriended years ago after rescuing him from a kidnapping. He didn't recognize him because the last time they had talked Ben's voice had been an octave higher.

"You aren't going to believe this, but she's finally doing it," Ben said. "Mom and Steve are getting married."

Louis leaned closer to the phone.

"Anyway, it's nothing fancy. You know Mom, she's not even going to change her name."

Well, what woman named Susan Outlaw would? Especially since she was a public defender. The fact that Steve's last name was Fuchs might have figured into her decision. Despite that, Louis had to admit Steve was a good man. And he'd make a good stepfather for Ben. Still, it stung a little to know that Ben just didn't seem to need him as much as he used to.

The next message on the machine began with a gruff cough.

"Yeah, this is Ned Willis, and this call is for Louis Kincaid, the private investigator."

Willis...the district attorney on the fraud case he had just finished down in Bonita Springs.

"You were set to testify next week but the trial has been postponed," Willis said. "We've rescheduled for September 3 but we definitely still need you to be here. My office will follow up with a letter. Thanks."

The next voice was female, flat and all too familiar.

"You have no more messages."

Louis stared at the machine for a moment then reset it to record. He got a fresh Heineken from the refrigerator, picked up the stack of mail and went out onto the screened-in porch.

Issy was curled on the lounge chair and he set her gently aside before he sat down. He took a long draw from the Heineken as he sorted through the mail. The stack was fat with supermarket flyers, bills, a Lillian Vernon catalog — how the hell had he gotten on that mailing list? — bank and credit card statements, and two copies of *Police* magazine.

He set the bills in one pile, gave the *Police* cover a quick glance and tossed the Lillian Vernon catalog to the floor. Something bright fluttered out.

A postcard. A postcard showing a horse and buggy.

Oh shit...

He retrieved the card but he didn't need to look at the back. He knew who it was from. With a sigh, he turned it over.

> Hi Louis,
> I found this card at the farmer's market. It's Mackinac Island! Isn't it funny that I found it here and it's the exact same place where we're going to go for my birthday? You don't have to give me a present. You can take me on a buggy ride instead. I can't wait to see you! – Lily

Louis looked out over the gulf. The sun was starting to set, leaving a pink smudge in the heat-hazed yellow sky.

Lily's birthday was September 2 and he had promised her he would come up to Michigan and take her to Mackinac Island. But now the damn fraud trial had been postponed and he had to be here instead.

Shit. Shit, shit...shit!

He felt eyes on him and looked down to see Issy looking up at him.

"What?" he said.

The cat just stared at him.

"Yes, I know," he said. "I'm a fuck-up. I'm a fuck-up who can't be bothered to pay attention to a cat let alone a kid."

Issy jumped off the lounge and went into the cottage. With sigh, Louis looked at the postcard again.

Until just a few months ago, he hadn't even known he had a daughter. Lily's mother Kyla had been an on-and-off girlfriend during his senior year at University of Michigan. The night she came to his dorm to tell him she was pregnant was etched in his memory like a bad dream.

Rain pounding on the window. Kyla standing at the door of his dorm room, so soaked from the rain he didn't even notice the tears running down her face.

I'm pregnant, Louis.

What do you want from me, Kyla?

I want to know you love me. I want to know you'll be there for me.

He didn't tell her what he was thinking. That he was twenty years old and he didn't want his life to be over. He just wanted — after too many foster homes, too many years bouncing from one place and face to another — he just wanted a clear smooth road ahead for a change.

Kyla's last words to him that night still stung.

I'll get rid of it then.

And his words stung worse.

Go ahead.

Louis stared at Lily's looped signature. Lily...just Lily. That was always how she signed the cards. What did he expect? Love, Lily?

Lily. Just Lily.

Kyla couldn't have known, of course. Couldn't have known that the name she had given to their daughter was a hybrid of her own name and that of Louis's dead mother Lila. Strange that the two females in his life who were like strangers to him had blended into this third little female who was becoming...

Becoming what?

His daughter?

He wasn't a father. Not yet. He had a long way to go to earn that title. He had no idea what it was going to take right now but he had the strange feeling it was going to be like running the tactical course, a series of twists and turns where things would come flying out of the blue and you never knew what was going to hit you and lay you low.

He downed the last of the beer. The low slant of the sun told him it was maybe six-thirty. Still plenty early enough to call Ann Arbor.

He gathered up the mail and went back inside. Setting the mail by the phone, he dialed Kyla's number but it went to the answering machine. He had a vague memory of the last time he had phoned and Lily telling him she was going to ballet camp in Interlochen sometime in August.

Damn.

Breaking the news to Lily that he wasn't going to make it for her birthday was not something he could leave in a message so he hung up. He'd try again in a couple days.

He stared at the steady red light of the answering machine, thinking now of Mel and Ben.

He thought, too, about the small group of people who circled in his life's orbit. Dan Wainwright, the first chief he had worked with when he moved to Fort Myers. Dan had retired two years ago and moved to Arizona. And Sam and Margaret Dodie, the older couple who treated him like a son but lately only seemed to call on holidays. And his foster parents Phillip and Frances. Even his contact with them had dwindled. Last time he talked to them — was it a month ago or two? — they had bought a new Airstream and were planning to wend their way toward Yosemite.

Everyone was moving on with their lives, moving away from him.

Even Joe.

Especially Joe.

After she left her job at Miami homicide to take the sheriff's job up in northern Michigan, they hadn't managed to make good on their promises to visit each other. When he had called her last Christmas, she had said that maybe they should see other people. It wasn't just the two thousand miles that separated them, he knew. It was the widening hole in his own life. Joe had put words to it.

I want you to want something for yourself. Louis.

And her unspoken words — and until you do I don't want you.

He grabbed the receiver and dialed Joe's cabin. He got the machine and hung up without leaving a message. When he dialed Joe's private number at the Leelanau County Sheriff's Department her secretary answered.

"This is Louis Kincaid," he said. "Is the Sheriff still there?"

"No, I'm sorry, she's not."

Louis shifted to look at the clock on the stove. It was nearly seven. Joe was probably on her way home.

"Do you want to leave a message?" the secretary asked.

"No, thanks. I'll try her at home."

"Oh, she's not there. She won't be back in town until next Monday."

Louis shifted the receiver to his other ear.

"Would you like to leave a message mister —"

"Kincaid. Louis Kincaid. No, no message." He started to hang up. "Wait, can you tell me where she went?"

The secretary hesitated.

"I'm a good friend," Louis said.

"Yes, Mr. Kincaid, I know who you are." She hesitated again. "The sheriff is on vacation. In Montreal."

Montreal?

"She'll be calling in to get messages, Mr. Kincaid," the secretary said. "I can tell her you called."

"What? No, no, that's okay," Louis said.

He thanked the secretary and hung up. He stood for a moment, staring into the deepening shadows of the living room, still wrapped in only the towel, his skin sticky from sweat. Finally, he moved to the air conditioner and flicked it on. With a groan, it began to split out a meager stream of cool air.

He grabbed the holstered Glock and went into the bedroom. It was nearly dark and he had to switch on the bedside light. He paused before he put the gun away, taking a moment to slip it from its holster.

The Buddha was in his head now, whispering.

For those of you who ride alone it is the only partner you'll ever have.

Damn it. He was getting tired of riding alone.

He slid the Glock back in the holster, put it in the drawer and went to the bathroom. His hands still smelled of Hoppes oil and he washed them quickly.

The smell was still there.

That's when he remembered it.

He opened the medicine chest, scanned the bottles on the shelves but it wasn't there. He jerked open the door beneath the sink and rummaged through the bottles of hydrogen peroxide, shampoo and shaving cream. He found it behind the rolls of toilet paper.

He rose, staring at the plastic bottle of Jean Naté After Bath Splash. It looked empty. He took off the top and upended the bottle into his palm. A trickle of green spilled out.

Louis brought his palms up to his nose and closed his eyes.

For a moment Joe was there and then she was gone.

CHAPTER SEVEN

They seem to be doing a very meticulous job."

Louis watched the two crime scene techs as they worked their way the through tangled brush, sticking evidence flags in the ground, taking pictures and sifting through the dirt.

He looked to Katy. She wore a green long-sleeved shirt over an old t-shirt, a vest bulging with stuffed pockets and long camouflage pants. Her face was streaked with sweat.

"The sheriff said they're the best techs he has," Louis said.

She looked up at the sky. "I hope they're quick," she said. "It's going to rain soon."

He glanced up at the sky. Ugly purple clouds were building to the southwest and the humid air was heavy with the smell of ozone. It wasn't just going to rain. It was going to be a palmetto-pounder of a storm.

Katy wandered away from him, apparently not expecting a reply. Although they were fifty feet from the techs, her eyes were also locked on the ground. Louis knew she was hoping she would find something the techs didn't. He understood that. Many times he had been at a scene, separated from the forensics team by yellow tape, but still he looked for something he thought only he could see.

Katy stopped under a tree and pulled off her ball cap to redo the scrunchie holding her ponytail. What a strange woman, he thought, quiet, reserved, somewhat disconnected from what was going on around her.

They had been together nearly two hours, walked maybe a mile, but she had spoken only three times. Once to ask how many days the techs would be able to come out here and once to caution him not to step on a Scarlet King snake. The third time she had stopped Louis and pointed to something up in a tree. His heart quickened because he thought he was going to see a panther but then he realized she was pointing to a purple and yellow flower high on a limb. She told him it was a rare clamshell orchid and like the panthers, the orchids were protected from poachers.

She was smiling — the first time he had seen her do so — so he just nodded, deciding not to tell her he already knew that. He had learned all about wild orchids from the weird case he had just finished over in Palm Beach, a string of grisly murders involving rich salacious women who all had an obsession with a rare flower called the Devil Orchid.

He thought about telling her about the case because he wanted to convince her that he wasn't just some hack PI trying to catch a chance with the sheriff's department. For some reason, he felt the need to impress this woman.

That's why he had gotten up early and stopped off at the Fort Myers Library. He had spent a quick hour reading everything he could find on Florida panthers.

The big cats, he learned, had once roamed over all of the southeast states and were hunted as pests, with the State of Florida offering a five-dollar bounty for every dead panther. As the state's human population grew, the panthers declined, their habitat shrunk by housing developments, highways and drainage canals. By the 1970s, everyone thought the animal was extinct.

But a Texas animal tracker named Roy McBride found evidence of surviving panthers. School kids took up the cause and pressured legislators to name the panther the state animal. Speed limits on the highways cutting through the Everglades were lowered and committees were created to save the cats.

It was an uphill battle. Only a handful of the cats were believed to still be alive and the ones that survived were weakened by inbreeding. Last year, in an act of desperation, the state had even started a sperm bank for the remaining males.

Louis had found one other interesting fact in a magazine article — the panther was considered sacred to the Seminole Indians.

Louis had read all this with a deepening sense of depression. But it also created in him a more urgent resolve. He was damned if he was going to let Mobley sideline this case.

"Kincaid!" one of the techs called. "Come here."

Louis started over toward Mickey, the older of the two techs. Katy hurried to catch up. They paused in a small clearing where the brush was tamped down into the muck.

"I have tire tracks," Mickey said.

Louis bent over but could see no definable impressions in the mess of leaves and mud. Mickey motioned for Louis to step back and pulled a clunky-looking light from his bag. He told his partner to hold a small tarp over the ground to block the sunlight and knelt down. When he directed the ultra-violet beam at the ground the rugged outlines of the tire tracks seemed to rise up from the mud. They were too narrow to have come from one of Fish and Game's giant swamp buggies.

"I'll know for sure later," Mickey said, "but I think we're looking at Super Swamper radials."

"Are they standard on a specific four-wheel drive?"

Mickey shut the light off and stood up. "No," he said. "People buy them for their mud buggies to be able to get around out here and any place else they want to go four-wheeling."

"But if we find a suspect we can compare his vehicle tires to these tracks?" Katy asked.

"That's the idea," Mickey said. "These treads look to be pretty worn with some specific nicks. If we find a suspect tire the match will be as strong as fingerprints, ma'am."

"How far do the tire tracks go?" Louis asked.

"Well, they look visible quite aways out heading toward the southeast."

Louis turned in the direction Mickey was pointing. He peered between the cypress trees to the prairie beyond. He was disoriented by the primitive landscape, not able to tell where the hell they were.

"What towns are we near?" he asked.

"Immokalee's the only one out here," Mickey said.

Louis nodded. At least he knew where that was. Once again, he had met up with Katy there, leaving his Mustang in Juan's parking lot. But Immokalee was to the northwest, in the opposite direction of these tire tracks.

The sun slipped behind some clouds and there was a low rumble of thunder.

"What else is out here?" Louis asked.

"There's some cattle ranches but they're pretty far east, closer to Lake Okeechobee, down around Devil's Garden," Mickey said.

Louis had been to Devil's Garden for the Palm Beach case. There was nothing there but a rusty sign marking an intersection, an old cinderblock store called Mary Lou's and an abandoned cattle pen where they had found a decapitated body. Devil's Garden and the cattle ranches were too far away for the panthers to be any threat to livestock.

"Actually, the closest thing to civilization way out here is the rez."

Louis looked back at the tech. "The Seminole reservation?" he asked.

"Yeah. It's called the Big Cypress Reservation."

"How far?"

"Oh, maybe twenty miles or so."

Louis glanced at Katy. She was slowly moving away, eyes still trained on the ground. There had been no accusing tone in Mickey's voice but Louis sensed Katy had heard something that had compelled her to step away from them and maybe away from the idea that an Indian might be involved. Louis decided to let the possibility go for now and hoped they would find something that led away from the reservation.

"Let's follow the tracks some," Mickey said.

He led Louis and Katy across the clearing, stabbing the ground with the small orange flags as he walked. Mickey stopped walking and knelt down. Drawing a small ruler from his shirt pocket, he measured the depth of the track in three places before looking up at Louis.

"The tracks deepen here by a quarter inch and look to continue that way," Mickey said, pointing south. "I'm guessing he stopped here and added weight to his load."

"Weight? How much weight?" Louis asked.

"Hard to say. Maybe a hundred pounds."

"He put Grace in his truck," Katy said.

"Grace?" the tech said.

"That's the missing panther's name," Louis said.

"I thought they just had numbers."

Katy turned to stare hard at the tech. "They do have numbers. She was FP105," she said dryly. "She weighed ninety-two pounds last time we were able to dart her and check."

Louis looked down. "If he loaded her up here, aren't we walking all over his footprints?"

"Already checked," Mickey said. "Foot prints would've been shallower, easily washed away by last night's rain."

"It didn't rain last night," Louis said.

"It did out here," Mickey said. "I checked before I left the station this morning. We're lucky he has Super Swampers on his vehicle or we might've lost these tracks, too."

"Hey Mick."

The other tech, a pudgy guy named Buck, appeared out of the brush. He wore a white paper jumpsuit, purple latex gloves and a pair of glass-es with a magnifying lens inset on the right side. He looked a little like a Haz-mat responder.

"Look what I got," he said.

He held up a clear plastic evidence bag. Inside was a slightly crumbled pack of cigarettes.

"It was back there, under a tree," Buck said. "I might be able to get some prints off it. Cellophane looks clean."

"Butts?" Louis asked.

"Nope," Buck said. "Haven't seen one butt of any brand."

"Can I see that?" Katy asked.

Buck handed the bag to her. She took a long look then handed the evidence bag back to Louis. She turned and walked away.

Louis stared at her back for a moment then brought the evidence bag up to peer closely at the pack inside. He could easily make out the brand — Viceroy — but it took him a couple more seconds to see what Katy had noticed. Cigarettes packs in Florida, as in all states, bore a state tax stamp on the bottom of the cellophane. This pack had no stamp and that meant one thing. It had come from the only place in the state where cigarettes weren't taxed — the reservation.

"I'll be right back," he said to Buck, handing him the bag.

He walked to where Katy stood. She had taken off her hat and wiped her face with her sleeve, leaving a dirty smear of sweat across her forehead.

"He's not Indian," she said.

"You don't know that," Louis said.

"I know," she said. "I feel it in here." She put her fist to her chest.

Louis took a slow breath. "Katy, I have to consider all possibilities or I'm not doing my job," he said.

"It is not your job anymore," she said. "I don't need you. I don't want you here anymore."

He stared at her in disbelief. He knew the Seminoles, much like the illegal Hispanics in Immokalee, resented outsiders even when they wanted to help. And he respected that. But she had invited him in her world, her uncivilized world of poisonous snakes, rare orchids and panthers that perched in trees. She had introduced him to the cats and somehow, just by the way she spoke of them, she had made them almost human.

He didn't want to walk away from this. He wanted to find Grace and he wanted to find her alive. Not just for Katy, but for himself. It was going to be his way back in.

"Take your techs and leave," Katy said. "I will find another investigator."

She turned and walked away from him, her step quickening as she neared her swamp buggy.

"Katy. Stop."

Without a look back, she climbed into the high seat of the buggy and started it up. The roar split the silence and the tech guys looked up in surprise. Then the big buggy rumbled away into the brush, leaving only the retreating growl of its engine in the sticky air.

CHAPTER EIGHT

Louis picked up the laundry basket, used a foot to slam the dryer door shut and headed back to his cottage.

He was coming around the rain-puddled yard when he saw the Game and Wildlife truck parked near the Branson's on the Beach sign. A moment later, Katy came off his porch, stopping short when she saw him.

"Oh, you're here," she said. "The door's open but there was no answer when I knocked."

"I was around back doing my laundry." He came onto the porch. "Come on in."

Inside, he set the basket on the counter. When he turned to Katy she was standing awkwardly just inside the living room. His radio was tuned to a classic rock station out of Tampa. Procol Harum's *Whiter Shade of Pale* was playing.

"I came here to apologize," she said.

"What for?"

"Leaving you stranded out in the slough this morning."

"I got a lift back with Mickey and Buck."

She gave a curt nod. She looked uncomfortable, like she wanted to say something else but didn't know how to begin.

"I was just going to have a beer," he said. "Want one?"

She nodded and ventured further into the living room, looking around. "Nice place," she said.

He nodded toward the plastic bucket he had set by the stove before he ducked into the refrigerator. "The roof leaks, there's no water pressure and the A/C is shot. Other than that, it's paradise." He handed her a beer. "Let's go out on the porch. It's cooler out there."

Katy settled into the old chaise so Louis took the wicker chair. She was quiet, sipping her beer as she looked out at the pale smudge of sun sinking slowly into the bank of rain clouds over the gulf.

"You've got a great view," she said finally, using her beer bottle to point to the swaying sea oats.

"Like I said, paradise," Louis said.

"Okay, this is tacky but I gotta ask. How do you afford a beach house on Captiva working as a PI?"

"Well, you are looking at the head of security for Branson's on the Beach," Louis said. "I get all the laundry tokens I can use and a break on the rent. All I have to do is make sure the kids don't play their radios too loud, check the locks on the empty cabins and make sure the trash can lids are shut to keep the raccoons out."

"How come you're working for Mobley?"

Louis took a drink before he answered. "I'm trying to get a job on the force. Your panther case is a kind of a test."

She considered him for a moment before she took a long draw on the beer. "How long you been doing PI work?" she asked.

"About four years. Sort of fell into it after I moved down here from Michigan."

Katy's gaze wandered back to the water. "Man, I'd love to live near the water," she said softly. "I share a shitty apartment with a roommates out near the Miromar outlet mall. I have a great view of I-75 from my bedroom and one shelf in the refrigerator."

"How long you been in Florida?" Louis asked.

"Thirty-three years. I'm a native."

This morning, when he brought up the Seminole angle Katy had almost bit his head off. He was almost sure she was Indian but there was no easy way to bring it up.

In his five years as a Florida PI he'd never had any direct contact with either the Seminoles or Miccosukees, the two surviving tribes in Florida. All he knew was that they ran a high-stakes bingo hall on the reservation west of Fort Lauderdale and were pressuring Florida politicians to open a real casino. They also sold the tax-free cigarettes at smoke shops scattered over on the east coast. And like all tribes, they were sovereign nations, exempting them from the normal reach of the law. They policed their own, with their own cops, courts and moral codes.

As Katy looked out over the water, Louis took the moment to study her.

She was dressed in baggy white linen clam-diggers, orange flip-flops and a blue t-shirt so faded he could barely make out the lettering on the front -- BOB SEGER AMERICAN STORM TOUR 1986.

There were no angles to her profile, except maybe the high plateau of her cheekbones on her round face. Her skin was smooth and almost the same light brown tone as his own. He hadn't really noticed her hair before now because she had always stuffed it up in her ball cap. But he could see it now, a long straight black sweep as magnificent as a thoroughbred's tail. Except for her hair clip, the only adornment she wore was a bracelet made of small blue and red glass beads.

He focused on the bracelet as she raised the beer to her lips.

"I like your bracelet," he said. "Is it Indian?"

Her eyes, when she turned to him, were as black and still as the slough water. "Yeah, it's Seminole," she said. "So am I."

Louis took a drink of beer. "I didn't mean to offend you this morning."

"You didn't."

Lightening zigzagged silently over the gulf. It was quiet except for the music coming from the radio inside.

"Oh man, I love this song," Katy said.

Louis strained to listen but he couldn't recognize it. That's why he liked this Tampa station. It played the obscure stuff.

"What is it?" he said.

"'Pretty as You Feel'."

It took him another full stanza before he recognized the singer's distinctive contralto. Another couple bars of the song before he made the other connection.

"Grace Slick," he said.

Katy looked over at him with a sly smile.

"And the other panther is named after Bruce Springsteen?" he asked.

She raised her beer in a salute.

Louis sat back in the wicker chair, propping his legs up on the table. "Why do you name them?" he asked.

She gave a small shrug. "So they aren't just numbers."

They were quiet until the song ended.

"I was reading about panthers today," Louis said. "I saw something that said they are sacred to the Seminoles."

It was getting dark and he couldn't see Katy's face. But she had relaxed some, her body sort of melting into the lounge. Whether it was from the beer or from being more comfortable around him he didn't know.

"Sacred," she said softly.

He waited.

"My great aunt used to tell me stories," she said. "They were like our fairy tales or like the Greeks making up stories to explain things that couldn't be explained." She looked over at him. "You want to hear one?"

"Please."

"Well, the Creator made all the animals but he loved the panther best," she said. "The panther would sit beside him and he would pet its soft furry back."

Katy took a drink of beer, her eyes going back out over the darkening gulf.

"When the Creator was making the earth, he put the animals in a large shell, telling them that when the time was right they would all crawl out," she went on. "He told the panther that because he was the most majestic and patient of all animals he was the perfect one to walk the earth first. Then he sealed up the shell and left."

"What happened?" Louis asked, when she didn't go on.

"A tree grew next to the shell and its roots cracked the shell open but no animals came out," Katy said. "The panther was patient, too patient. So the wind, which knew the Creator wanted the panther to come out first, blew on the shell so hard the crack grew larger and the panther came out. Then all the other animals came out too."

She laid her head back on the lounge.

"The Creator watched all this and decided to put all the animals into clans," she said. "For being his faithful companion, the creator gave the panther with special qualities. Your clan, he said, will have knowledge of all special things. You will have the power to heal."

Louis had a vague memory from his research, something about the Seminoles being divided into clans.

"Do your people still have clans?" he asked.

She seemed surprised by the question. "Yeah, we do," she said. "Your clan is inherited through your mother. There used to be more clans but many went extinct. There are only eight left — panther, bear, deer, wind, bird, snake, otter and Big Town."

"Big Town?"

"It was created for non-Indian women. The myth is that during the Seminole wars in the eighteen-hundreds, two white girls were found wandering in the woods. The Seminoles took them in but because they didn't have Indian mothers, they could belong to no clan. So one was created for them."

It was dark now. The signal from the Tampa station had faded, the music a dull murmur of static drowned out by the surf's whisper.

And then, a plaintive meow.

Louis sat up, looking to the screen door. Issy's black form was just visible outside. He rose and held the door open. The cat came onto the porch, pausing to look up at Katy.

"You have a cat?" she said.

"I told you I did."

Issy came to her, arching her back against Katy's leg. Katy set her beer bottle down and bent low, running her hand over the cat's sides.

"What's her name?"

"Issy."

The cat suddenly bounded off into the cottage.

"Well, I think it's time for me to go," Katy said.

When she awkwardly tried to extricate herself from the lounge, Louis rose quickly and helped her to her feet. He reached inside the door and slapped the porch light switch. When Katy headed toward her truck, he followed.

She paused at her truck's door, turning toward him.

"I thought you were bullshitting me about having a cat," she said.

"I'm not much of a bullshitter."

Her face, reflected in the porch light, was unreadable. She got in the truck but turned to him, elbow on the open window.

"Look," she said. "I spent all day thinking about this. I still don't think a Seminole would harm a panther but I am willing to let this investigation go where it needs to go. I want to find Grace and I want you to stay on the case. Do you want to?"

"Yes," Louis said. "Call me in the morning and we'll talk about our next move."

She gave him a nod and started the truck.

"Your cat is really thin," she said.

"I know."

"How old is she?"

"I don't know." Louis hesitated. "I'm worried she dying."

"Old cats get thyroid disease," Katy said. "She'll probably be okay with meds. Have her tested, okay?"

Before Katy could leave, Louis put a hand on the open window.

"Can I ask you something personal?" he said.

"Sure."

"What clan do you belong to?"

She hesitated. "Snake."

"Not my first guess," he said.

She gave him an odd smile and jammed the truck into drive, pulling out of the yard.

Louis watched until the tail lights disappeared down Captiva Drive then went back into the cottage. Issy was waiting by her empty bowl in the kitchen. He poured a bag of Tender Vittles into her bowl and sat at the counter, watching her as she ate.

When she was finished, he picked her up, grabbed a fresh beer and went back to the porch. There he sat, watching the silver curtain of rain move in from Gulf and stroking Issy's thinning fur.

CHAPTER NINE

The thing was lying in the middle of the road.

At first Louis thought it was a big log but after he slowly moved the Jeep ahead, he hit the brakes hard.

Alligator. It was a damn alligator.

It was at least twelve feet long and it was sprawled straight across the width of the dirt road.

Louis inched closer until the tires were almost touching the thing. It didn't move.

Louis stood up in the seat and scanned the sides of the road but the brush was too thick and soggy so there was no way to turn around. And by his calculations he had left the paved road at least five miles back so he wasn't about to go back all that way in reverse.

He had been out here for almost two hours already, driving around in circles in the open vehicle. He had a headache from the sun baking his head and his kidneys felt like they were going to fall out from all the jostling. He wasn't sure he was even on the right road.

He looked back at the gator and laid hard on the horn.

The thing still didn't budge. Didn't even move a slitted eye in his direction.

Fuck!

He looked in the back for something he could throw. Nothing but a big empty Coleman cooler. He had a water bottle but he wasn't about to sacrifice that. There was probably a jack and crowbar somewhere but he'd be damned if he was going to get out and look. He glanced down at the holster on the passenger seat. With one eye on the gator, he slipped out the Glock, pointed it at the dirt and fired.

The alligator gave a loud hiss and slithered off into the brush.

Louis holstered the Glock, sat back down behind the wheel and continued down the rutted dirt road.

This trip had seemed like a good idea this morning when he went into the station to pick up the four-wheel drive Mobley had promised him.

The cop manning the desk in the garage was named Sergeant Sweet, but he had given Louis the same sour look all the cops had been giving him. The rogue PI, riding his way into the department on an EEOC horse. That's what they all thought. Sweet asked Louis if he was "working the panther thing."

When Louis said he was, the sergeant said his ten-year-old daughter had started a petition in her class to get the Florida panther named the state animal and she was sad about the one that had gone missing.

"Find the damn cat," the sergeant said. "I don't want to have to tell my kid the thing is dead."

Then he handed over the keys to a souped-up Jeep that had been commandeered from a drug raid and told Louis that he should check out "the weirdos out in the swamp camps."

There were hundreds of hunting camps on private land in the Everglades, the sergeant explained. After the federal government created the preserves in the seventies, the camps were grandfathered in and a handful still existed, handed down from one generation to the next.

Most were down south of I-75 but there was one just a few miles from where Grace had disappeared, the sergeant said. It was called Hell's Hammock.

Be careful, he added, they're all mouth-breathers who love their guns and hate the government. And that includes anyone wearing a badge.

Louis hadn't told anyone else where he was going. He hadn't even called Katy.

It wasn't just the fact that the swamp camp men were bound to be hostile to a strange black man let alone a woman ranger. He was shutting her out for now because this was his world — going after dirt bags in a possibly dangerous situation. She didn't belong here.

He would tell her later. His plan right now was simple: just quietly look around and check these guys out.

If he could find them.

Sergeant Sweet wasn't sure exactly where Hell's Hammock was. The directions were vague, just land-marks mainly. About halfway across I-75, he was supposed to watch for a gravel service road just past the first rest stop. Louis had found the road but deep into a jungle of palmetto palms it began to narrow. The brush created a tunnel so thick and close Louis had to shift in the seat toward the middle to keep from getting scraped.

The road forked and dead-ended a couple times, forcing Louis to back up and look for landmarks he had missed. The sergeant had said to watch for an American flag tied to a tree and turn left, but the only thing hanging from trees out here was Spanish moss.

Damn. Another dead-end. And this one looked like he wasn't even going to be able to back out. He glanced down at the police radio on the seat but the signal had died miles ago.

He downshifted and eased the Jeep forward. There was a patch of sunlight ahead. And a tatter of a faded old flag hanging limp from a tree.

After a left turn, the thicket opened into a small clearing. He went another twenty yards then stopped, taking stock. There were three buildings, crudely made from plywood and topped with tin roofs. The largest of the three had a sagging porch and small windows covered with shutters. The other two buildings were small, probably a storage shed and an outhouse. There were no vehicles of any kind to be seen.

And no sign of a human being.

Except...the front door of the main building was wide open.

Louis turned off the Jeep. In the quiet that piled in he could hear the whisper of the pines that ringed the compound and then the cry of a swallow-tail kite.

Maybe the men were out hunting. He got out of the Jeep, scanning the ground for tracks but saw nothing in the dirt and long grass. In fact, except for the open door, the camp looked deserted.

He had a sudden flashback to walking into another camp. It was years ago and thousands of miles away. Northern Michigan, in the dead of winter, and he was hunting a cop killer. The trail had led him to a remote camp inhabited by off-the-grid Vietnam vets. A one-armed soldier named Cloverdale had held him at bay with an AK47, endured his questions, then sent him back down the snowy hill with a warning never to come back.

Louis reached into the Jeep and got his Glock. He slipped it into the large front pocket of his khaki vest. If anyone was here, he thought as he started for the open door, he didn't want them to think he was a cop. He'd be run off, or worse, before he ever got his first question out.

At the open door, he paused. As far as he could see in the dim interior, there was no one inside. It was one big room, maybe twenty-four by fifteen feet. He could make out the outlines of a table and chairs, some bunk beds and what looked like a primitive kitchen.

He stepped inside.

The door slammed closed behind him. Something hard and heavy came down on the back of his head. Stunned and seeing white, he fell forward. His hands skid over rough wood, his palms ripped with splinters.

"Hit him again, man! Hit him again!"

Louis tried to turn over but a boot slammed into his back. Then again into his shoulder and a third time into the back of his head. His hands flew up to protect his head but suddenly someone was on him, punching him and groping at his pockets.

"Get his wallet! Get his fucking money!"

Louis started swinging, feeling his fists hit flesh but the man on top of him didn't budge.

It was getting hard to breathe and there was blood in his eyes. He felt the man's hands roughly moving down his chest. They stopped when they got to the bulge of the Glock.

"He's got a fucking gun!"

Louis grabbed at him, trying to keep him from getting to the Glock. The man punched him hard in the face. A flash of white light then he felt himself going out. Flicking light and voices cutting in and out, like a bad radio connection.

Stay awake...stay awake...

The man was suddenly gone but Louis couldn't move. He could barely breathe. There was a fire in his side and he knew his ribs were broken.

"Look at this, it's a fucking Glock. It's gotta be worth five hundred easy."

"Where we gonna sell it? Tell me that, Memo! We can't go back to Lauderdale. We can't go nowhere now after what you did."

"The fucker wouldn't give me the money!"

"He didn't have any fucking money! It was already in the safe!"

Quiet. The voices were quiet for a second.

"Get his wallet."

Louis tried to get up. He had to fight. He had to —

"Don't be stupid, man. I got your Glock pointed at your head."

Crushing pressure of a boot on his back was holding him down. More hands digging into the back pocket of his jeans.

"Got it. He's got thirteen bucks and a VISA card."

"Check the other vest pockets for the Jeep keys," the other man said.

The boot came off his back and one of the men rolled him onto his back.

Two faces blurry above him — one pale and long, the other dark and round. Ball caps, dirty t-shirts, jeans caked with mud. The dark man was padding him down and Louis fought back his rise of panic. If they found the badge he was a dead man.

"Got the keys." The man's hands stopped. "Hey, he's got another wallet."

Louis felt the guy pull out the small leather wallet that Mobley had given him.

"He's a cop!"

"What?"

"Look at this, Marv. He's a fucking cop."

The pale man's eyes went from the badge down to Louis.

"How'd you find us, cop?"

Louis was silent.

"Where are the others?"

"No others," Louis mumbled. He felt blood in his mouth and spat it out. "I wasn't looking for you."

"We need to get out of here, Marv. Shoot the fucker and —"

"Shut up, Memo! I need to think."

Louis pushed to a sitting position and tried to focus on the two men. If he got out of this cabin alive he wanted to remember enough to catch these bastards.

Marv was six-foot and slender, shaved head, horsey face and prominent bad teeth. The t-shirt, Louis could see now, had a Harley emblem on it. The other guy, the one called Memo, was dark, Hispanic maybe, and gone to fat. His faded orange Miami Dolphins t-shirt had the sleeves cut off. He had a scorpion tattoo on his neck.

The bald guy tossed the badge wallet to the floor then leaned over and pressed the barrel of the Glock to Louis's temple.

"You kill me, you die in the chair," Louis said.

The man's breath was like sewer water. "I don't like niggers and I don't like cops."

He eased the Glock away from Louis's head. He threw the badge wallet into a corner. "But I ain't no murderer."

He moved away. Louis shut his eyes in relief. He could hear the creak of the floorboards as the man moved around the room.

"Find something to tie him up with."

Louis watched the dark man as he rummaged through the kitchen. When he came back, Louis saw a loop of old rope in his hands. The bald man pointed the Glock toward the bunk beds.

"Move your ass over there."

Louis crawled to the bunks. They were heavy wooden things, built into the wall. He leaned back against a post, his ribs on fire.

The dark man forced Louis's hands behind his back. Louis grimaced as the man wrapped the rope tight around his wrists, tying it off high on the top bunk. The dark guy was smiling when he stepped back to admire his handiwork.

"Let's get out of here," the bald guy said.

The other man grabbed a backpack off the counter, paused, then reached over Louis to snag a pack of cigarettes from the bunk.

As they left, the dark guy started to pull the door closed. The bald man slapped a hand against it.

"Leave it open. Maybe a gator will crawl in and eat him."

Louis could hear them laughing until it was drowned out by the sound of the Jeep coming to life. It built to a roar as they revved the engine then slowly it faded to a low growl as they pulled out of the camp.

Louis strained against the rope. No give. His hands were going numb.

He looked to the open door, trying to estimate what time it was. He had signed out the Jeep at ten-thirty this morning but in all the twisting and turning trying to find this place he had lost track of time.

Sergeant Sweet...he was the only one who knew where he had gone. But there was no reason for him to sound the alarm if Louis didn't come back. The Jeep was signed out for indefinite use.

Louis tugged at rope. There was no give, n way to even stand up to get his weight behind him. He laid his head back against the post.

It was quiet. A terrible, empty quiet.

CHAPTER TEN

The darkness had crept over him — the rectangle of light that defined the open door turned from green to gray then disappeared — and he thought it was because he was losing consciousness. But then, out of the blackness, came sounds.

The soft whir of a motor.

The creak of a rusty hinge.

Coughing.

Had the men come back? He strained to see something, anything, in the pitch black.

No, no...

Just crickets, frogs, and something else, a gator maybe.

Louis leaned back against the bunk. How long had he been here? He couldn't tell anymore. It was the thick of night now and any hope he had of someone finding him was fading fast. It hurt to take a breath and he had to piss. He twisted his hands but the rope held tight on his wrists, cutting into his skin.

There was nothing to do but wait for the light. Maybe he could chew through the rope. Maybe if he yelled someone would be close enough to hear. Maybe...

He would die here.

He closed his eyes.

The rectangle of the door materialized out of the gloom. Dawn. His ribs and his lip throbbed. His parched throat felt like sandpaper and his whole body ached. Had he slept? He didn't know because his mind felt as numb as his hands. The gnawing in his stomach wasn't hunger anymore. It was fear.

He lay his head against the rough wood of the bunk, watching the details of the brush outside in the compound emerge in the frame of the doorway. He closed his eyes.

A sound. Close.

His eyes shot open. He jerked upright as far as the rope would allow.

An animal.

No! It was louder. And it was engine of some kind, he could tell now. It was getting louder. It was outside in the compound. Then, suddenly, it died and it was quiet.

Louis waited, his eyes riveted on the open door. A huge silhouette filled the doorframe.

"What the fuck?"

The voice was different from those of the two men who had left him here. Very deep, no accent. It took Louis a second to realize the man was holding a rifle. And it was aimed at Louis.

"Hey! Don't shoot!" Louis yelled.

The rifle kept its bead on Louis's chest.

"What the fuck are you doing here?"

"I've been here all night. Come on, untie me, man."

"This is my camp, asshole. You broke into my camp."

"I didn't break in. Two guys jumped me." No choice, he had to chance it. "I'm a cop, man. My ID is over there on the floor by the table."

Slowly the rifle came down. The man scooped up the wallet, glanced at the ID inside and looked back to Louis. "What are you doing in my camp?"

"Untie me. I'll explain."

The man set the rifle by the door and pulled a large knife from his belt. He knelt by Louis.

"Don't do anything stupid," he said as he began to saw at the rope.

"All I want to do is take a piss."

The rope snapped free. The man stepped back and picked up his rifle. Louis rubbed his wrists and holding his ribs, got to his feet. He walked unsteadily out the open door and unzipped his fly. When he was done, he looked back at the man who had come out to stand on the porch. He was a burly six footer with dark hair, dressed in old jeans and a denim shirt bleached almost to white. He had his rifle tucked un-der his arm and was looking at the police wallet. When his eyes came up to Louis they were hard.

"Louis Kincaid," he said, pronouncing his name Lou-ee. "Okay, what's your story Lou-ee Kincaid."

Louis pulled in a painful breath and launched into a quick summary of the panther case. When he was finished, the man shook his head and smiled.

"So you figured that some hunters killed your cat and you came out here to bust us, huh?"

"I don't know what I figured," he said. "You got some water?"

The man didn't move. "You know, it was stupid of you to come out here alone," he said. "I could have shot you."

"I know," Louis said, patting his swollen lip. "I should have told Katy I was coming here."

"Katy? Katy Letka?"

Louis looked up. "Yeah. Do you know her?"

"Yeah, I know Katy."

Louis stared at the man — he was smiling at the mention of Katy's name — as his fogged brain trying to make sense of this.

"You're a friend of Katy's?" the man asked.

"Yeah." Louis hesitated. "Are you?"

"Shit, yeah."

The man's eyes swept over Louis then he turned and went to his swamp buggy parked under the trees. He returned with a canteen and held it out to Louis.

Louis took it and drank greedily.

"So tell me about these guys who jumped you," the man said.

"Not much to tell," Louis said. "Like I said, they were hiding out in the cabin and jumped me when I came in."

"Someone's been using our camp," the man said. "I've been coming out here to check every couple days."

"I don't think these two are your guys," Louis said. "They were on the run from something they did over in Fort Lauderdale. They didn't seem too bright."

The man nodded. "Whoever's using my camp has been coming and going for months. We noticed it when we realized some canned food was missing."

Louis took another drink of water, trying not to gulp. His head was slowly clearing.

"One of my buddies got a glimpse of him once, but couldn't track him," the man said.

"What did he look like?"

"Stocky, dark-skinned, long black hair. He just disappeared into the swamp. He seems to know what he's doing out here. We call him the phantom. The only thing he leaves is cigarette butts."

"Cigarettes? You know what kind?" Louis asked.

"No, but the butts are probably out in the trash."

"Can you show me?"

Louis followed the man out to one of the small out-buildings and waited until the man unearthed a heavy black trash bag. Louis opened it, grimaced at the smell, but dug through it until he found a butt.

He squinted, unable to see a brand name on it without his reading glasses. "You see a name?" he asked, holding it out the man.

The guy came took it. "Viceroy."

Louis let out a painful breath.

"That mean something?" the man asked.

"Maybe. The guy who abducted the panther smokes Viceroys."

The man tossed the butt back in the trash and secured the lid. "Your ribs broken?" he asked Louis.

"I hope not."

"Well, we better get you someplace where we can find out."

Louis nodded and they started toward the swamp buggy. The seat was a good four feet off the ground and when Louis hesitated, holding his side, the man set his rifle in the back and helped Louis up into the seat.

"Thanks." Louis paused. "What's your name?"

"Gary. Gary Trujillo."

"Thanks, Gary."

The man jumped into the driver's seat and started the engine. The swamp buggy roared to life. Louis spotted a CB radio mounted on the dash.

"I need to get an APB out on the guys from Lauderdale," he said. "Can I use your radio?"

Gary pulled sunglasses out of his pocket and slipped them on. "You get a good look at the scum-bags?"

"Yeah," Louis said. He gave Gary a quick description.

Gary keyed the CB, calling someone named Otter. Louis listened as Gary described the two men who had violated their hunting camp and ordered a swamp buggy posse to hunt them down.

"We got it, Tru," Otter answered and signed off.

Gary put the swamp buggy in gear but before he pulled out he looked at Louis.

"We'll find the guys who did this to you," Gary said. "I only want one thing in return."

"What's that?"

"No publicity. We just want to be left alone, okay?"

Gary pulled out of the compound. Neither man said anything as Gary expertly maneuvered the buggy over the rutted roads. Louis sat silent, holding his ribs against the bouncing, thinking about what was going to happen if one of Gary's friends found the two men who had jumped him.

He didn't care. Marv and his little friend Memo had done something over in Lauderdale that was bad enough to drive them into the stinking bowels of the Everglades. And he knew that when the two dirt bags were caught — and as Louis looked over at Gary's profile he had no doubt they would be — Louis would get the credit for the collar of two fugitives.

"Gary," Louis shouted over the engine's din.

"What?"

"I can try to keep you and Otter out of things, but what if the scumbags talk about you?"

Gary gave him a crooked smile. "Don't worry. They won't."

CHAPTER ELEVEN

Four days, Kincaid," Mobley said. "Four days and already you've managed to get your name in the paper."

Louis looked beyond Mobley to the window, to the cloudless blue sky with its searing white sun. There was no way he could explain what had really happened out at the hunting camp. It was like something out of a James Dickey novel.

Marv had done exactly what Gary predicted: found the westward road that was paved enough to lull Marv into thinking he was on his way to Immokalee where he'd be able to fill his belly with beer and his head with hopes of making a clean getaway.

But Old Bucket Road was one of those roads Louis had gotten turned around on coming in. He had almost ended up in a ditch of black water and needed to slowly reverse his way out. Sure enough, that was where Otter had found the Jeep, only Marv had been too stupid to try to back up and had driven the Jeep door-high into a gator hole. When Otter and the other men surrounded the Jeep with rifles drawn, Marv and Memo, covered with mosquito welts and fear-sweat, had surrendered without a fight. By the time Gary and Louis arrived, the dirt bags were tied to a tree and Otter had pulled the Jeep from the bog. Louis's Glock was laying on the driver's seat.

"Remember our deal," Gary said. And he and the others were gone in a cloud of noise and gas fumes.

As soon as Louis was able to get radio contact driving back to Fort Myers, he informed the sheriff's dispatcher that he was en route with two fugitives from Fort Lauderdale. He made sure he used the frequency the local reporters monitored because even though he didn't really want the publicity he needed it. Needed everyone, not just Mobley, to see this notch his belt.

The WINK news truck was sitting in the sheriff's lot when Louis shoved the handcuffed Marv and Memo through the station doors. The story about a local PI, working for the sheriff's department, busting two fugitives who had robbed a 7-Eleven and sent the clerk to the hospital with a ruptured spleen was a big story on slow news day. By morning the papers had the story.

And this morning, when Louis walked in the station on his way to Mobley's office, for the first time the cops he passed gave him a nod of acceptance.

Louis looked from the window back to Mobley. It was hard not to smile.

"I don't believe you got me into something like this," Mobley said, tossing the *News Press* to the desk. "Who the fuck is going to believe this crap?"

"Look, sheriff, I told you the truth about what happened, but I don't think you really want the truth out there," Louis said. "They'll ridicule you over this whole lost cat thing and this good PR will go away."

Mobley ran a hand through his hair and turned his chair toward the window. Louis stayed standing, his gaze drifting to the newspaper. He hadn't mentioned something else to Mobley, a story he had read in the same paper while he waiting for Mobley to come in. An article on the upcoming EEOC civil trial Lee County was facing in federal court. Worse, there were whispers of a recall election for the sheriff in the wind at O'Sullivan's.

Mobley spoke without turning his chair. "Goddamn, you're a pain in my ass."

"We still got a deal?"

Mobley swung his chair around and gave Louis a long look. "Yeah," he said. "But now you need to bump these fucking Lauderdale shitheads out of the news cycle before some reporter starts digging deeper. You need to find me that cat."

"I'm working on it."

"You got any leads?"

"Maybe," Louis said. "The hunter told me there was a fellow hanging around the camp. He didn't get a good look at him but he said he was dark skinned with long black hair."

"That's it?"

"No, we found pack of cigarettes at Grace's crime site and I'm hoping to get prints off the cellophane, but the lab's taking its time. The cigarettes were purchased on the reservation."

"No tax stamp."

"Right."

"So, you're linking the smokes with this guy with the long black hair and thinking you might have a Seminole for a perp."

"There's another connection," Louis said. "The Seminoles believe the panther is the Creator's favorite animal and endowed with special powers —"

"Spare me the Jungle Book shit," Mobley said. "What you're telling me is that you want to take a trip to the rez and ask around about some weirdo who wanders the Glades and might be stealing the panthers, even though the damn cats are sacred to his tribe?"

"Yes, sir."

Mobley sighed. "Do you know how unwelcome we are there?"

"Yes."

"And you realize that even if the cat-napper pops out of a teepee with the damn cat on a leash, you have no authority there to arrest him?"

"I know that, too."

"Then why are you going?"

"I just want to ask some questions," Louis said. "I believe that if the panthers are as special as I've been told, I might get someone to talk to me."

Mobley was quiet, his eyes drifting to the newspapers before they came back to Louis. "Okay, but I want you to take an Indian with you."

"Excuse me?" Louis asked.

"I said, I want you to take an Indian with you so you don't get yourself shot or something," Mobley said. "I have one down in the traffic division. I'll call down and get him up here."

"No thanks, sir."

"Why the hell not?"

Louis paused, thinking of Katy. He had ignored her advice about the camps and got his ass kicked. Now he was about to ask her to help him go after one of her own people. No way she would help. But there was no way could he do this without her.

"I have my own Indian, sir," Louis said.

CHAPTER TWELVE

The smell wasn't strong but it was enough to take him back decades. Suddenly, he was eleven years old again and staring at a lion.

It was a very old lion but a lion nonetheless and he had been scared, hiding behind his foster father Phillip's leg. It was his first trip to the Detroit Zoo and the smell of the lion house was heavy in his nostrils, like nothing he had ever smelled before, like nothing he would ever smell again.

Until now.

Louis stood at the entrance of the room, his eyes roaming over the line of large cages to his left. All four were occupied by panthers, two lying down, two pacing. He wondered which one was Bruce but there were only numbers on the paperwork hanging on each cage and he couldn't remember Bruce's.

A door banged open at the far end and Katy came toward him. She was wearing a plastic apron over her uniform and a look of derision on her face.

She stopped before him, hands on hips. "You should have called me," she said.

"I know. Did you see it on TV?"

"No, Gary called me not long after he left you." She shook her head. "What the hell were you thinking going out there alone?"

"Look, Katy, I had reason to believe those guys at the hunting camps —"

"No you didn't!" She took a deep breath. "Those guys would never hurt a cat," she said. "They hunt, yeah, and they're a little off the grid, yeah. But they know more about the Glades and care more about the Glades and the animals there than any half-assed tree-hugger. Gary and his guys helped us get the panthers declared endangered, for God's sake."

She fell quiet. Louis noticed the two panthers had stopped pacing and were watching her.

"I'm sorry," Louis said. "I made an assumption about —"

"Yeah, cops tend to do that about people they don't know."

"I'm not a cop, Katy."

She was quiet. He was wondering how he was going to bring up going to the reservation. Wasn't that another assumption about people he didn't know much about?

"How's Bruce doing?" he asked finally.

"Come see for yourself." She led him to the last cage. Bruce was lying in the corner, his back leg splinted. The cat raised his big head to look at Louis then put it down again, closing his eyes.

"Is he okay?"

"Turned out it's just a bad sprain," Katy said. "But he's depressed. He wants to get out of here and go home."

Louis thought of his six hours in the emergency room last night waiting for the pimple-faced intern to send him on his way with a pain prescription and the pronouncement that there was no cure for his two bruised ribs except rest.

"I know how he feels," Louis said.

Katy looked up at him, eyeing his swollen lip. "Gary says they roughed you up pretty good."

Louis just nodded.

"You're damn lucky Gary came by."

Louis nodded again.

Katy let out a sigh and waved a hand. "Come on. Let's go to my office and talk about where we're going next."

Her office was a corner of a cramped room with file cabinets, four vacant desks, and walls covered with maps, photographs, and notices about the panther conservation program. One bulletin board showed photographs of school kids posing with a panther and the kids' hand-written notes and drawings of cats.

Katy moved a pile of files and motioned for Louis to take the chair next to her desk. She scanned a stack of message slips, tossed them down and swiveled her chair to face Louis.

"So what's our next step?"

Louis pulled in a breath so deep it hurt his ribs. "You aren't going to like it."

"I want Grace back. Try me."

Louis told her what Gary had said about the man breaking into the camp, adding the detail about the cigarettes with no tax stamp and the physical description Gary had provided. He watched her expression go from comprehension to a sort of weary sadness.

"You aren't thinking of going out to the rez alone, are you?" she asked.

"No."

Her eyes stayed on him for a moment then drifted off to something on the left. Louis saw it was a photograph of a panther. He couldn't be sure but he thought it looked like Grace. Katy blew out a long breath and rose, taking off the plastic apron and picking up her ball cap.

"Let's get going," she said.

The Seminole Indian reservation was located just off Alligator Alley – the old name for Interstate 75 that everyone used for the highway that cut an east-west slash across the Everglades.

The tribe had turned their access to the interstate into a profitable oasis that offered the only gas, food and reliably clean bathrooms for anyone traveling the hundred and fifteen miles between the South Florida coasts. If you wanted some entertainment, the Seminoles also provided airboat rides in the swamps, a tour of an authentic Indian village, a museum and an alligator wrestling show.

A couple miles north of that lay the real reservation. It was a simple grid of concrete block houses and trailers interrupted by the occasional store. Black-haired boys in t-shirts and Nikes played soccer in a dirt yard, chased by dogs. A knot of women, arms draped with plastic bags from Walmart and Publix, talked on a corner. Two men stood outside the open door of a cinderblock Baptist church smoking cigarettes. It looked like any of the hard-scrabble little towns that dotted the southwest Florida landscape.

"How's the tribe doing?" Louis asked.

Katy gave him a glance as she swung the Bronco down a side street. "Better than most, worse than some. They've made some money on cigarettes and bingo but the chief is pushing hard for a real casino. And I wouldn't bet against him."

Louis knew that Indian tribes all across the country were talking about casinos now. A mega-resort was planned for the lush Connecticut countryside and he had heard a Michigan tribe was also fighting to build one. Seeing the humble houses made him think that a business that employed a couple thousand people with benefits could do nothing but good for a place like this. But from the tone in Katy's voice, she didn't sound as if she approved.

"You don't want to see a casino here?" he asked.

"I'm not sure," Katy said. "It's sort of like winning the lottery. It doesn't always bring what you expect."

"Unemployment is high here, right?" Louis asked.

She nodded. "And too many of the kids drop out of school." She was quiet for a long time. "I was lucky. I got a scholarship from the tribe to FSU. But the money's dried up."

"Why?"

"I don't know," she said quietly. "I think they're afraid the kids won't come back."

Katy swung the Bronco around a corner and stopped in front of a one-story brick building with a colorful tribal seal mounted near the glass doors. They climbed from the Bronco but before Louis even closed the door, a man emerged from the building. He was well over six feet with the build of a wrestler and the posture of man ready to defend his territory. Short cropped black hair framed a face that told Louis he was close to forty and had sent a good part of his life in the Florida sun.

"Katy Letka," the man said.

Katy stopped a few feet in front of him. "Hello, Moses."

"It's been a long time. You look well."

"I am. You look well, too."

His black eyes shifted to Louis. "Who is this?"

"Louis Kincaid," Katy said. "He's working with the sheriff's office to help locate a missing panther. Louis, this is Moses Stanton, the tribal chairman's executive assistant."

Stanton studied Louis for a moment then turned back to Katy. "You are also looking for this panther?"

"Yes, I'm still with the Fish and Game department," she said. "And yes, I still love it."

"Your skills could be useful here."

Louis glanced at Katy. She suddenly seemed very stiff, staring at Moses Stanton with a hard squint. He suspected there might be more history here than just a tribal member who had left the flock.

"I'm useful where I am," Katy said.

"Then why are you here?" Stanton asked.

"The missing panther is a female," Katy said. "She has been gone four days now but she wasn't the only cat involved in whatever is going on. Before she was taken, a male panther turned up wounded. We think whoever took Grace tried to take the male panther but lost him."

"Capturing two large cats. Not an easy task."

"You're right," Katy said. "He would have to be someone who knows the Glades and is familiar with the panthers."

"He also has access to animal tranquilizers," Louis added.

Stanton gave Louis a dismissive glance before his eyes moved back to Katy. "So I ask you again, why are you here?"

"We have a description of a man who has been seen in the hunting camps," Katy said. "Long dark hair, brown skin, good at eluding the hunters."

"An Indian," Stanton said.

"Yes."

"No Indian would harm the panthers."

"I'm not sure he's looking to harm them," Katy said. "I believe he may be trying to mate them."

"For what purpose?"

"I don't know. I can only guess he thinks a cub will somehow bring him something he cannot otherwise obtain. Peace. Happiness. Some kind of special power maybe."

"He sounds like a crazy man," Stanton said.

"Most criminals are," Louis said.

This time Stanton didn't even look to Louis. His eyes drifted away from Katy to the street. He was quiet for a long time before he looked back to Katy.

"You have not been here to see your great aunt Betty in a long time," he said.

Katy looked suddenly stricken. She took a step toward Stanton as if trying to cut Louis off from hearing. "Does Betty ask about me?" she asked softly.

"No. She recognizes no one now. Your cousins sit around her bed and sing for her soul."

Katy pulled the brim of her ball cap lower and looked to the ground.

"The Alzheimer's is bad," Stanton said. "Her body is giving up. She is giving up."

Katy looked up. "Why didn't someone call me?"

"No one should have to."

Katy's face was slick with sweat. Louis could almost feel the heat of shame radiating off her.

"Katy," he said, "I'll go wait in the truck."

"No, wait," Katy said, grabbing his arm. She turned back to Stanton. "I will go to see Betty today, Moses. But right now, I need to talk about the panther. Please. I need, we need, your help."

Stanton didn't move a muscle. Then he looked over Katy to Louis, meeting his eyes. Louis had the weirdest feeling, like the man could almost read his thoughts. Like he could almost sense that the missing panther wasn't important to Louis, that it was just a means to an end. Louis forced himself to hold Moses's Stanton's stare.

"Moses," Katy said, "you know everything that goes on here. I need you to tell me if anyone has been acting strangely. Has anyone moved away and taken a home in the swamps? Have you caught anyone stealing supplies or drugs from the clinic?"

Moses finally broke his stare with Louis and crossed his arms. "I know no one who would interfere with the panthers. And I am not sure I would tell if I did."

"Moses," Katy said softly. "You know what they mean to me."

For the first time Louis detected a crack in the man's façade.

Stanton looked away toward the knot of kids kicking a soccer ball. "All right, Katy Letka," he said quietly. "I will help you. I will conduct my own investigation and if I find you are right, I will let you know so you can find the panther and take her back where she belongs."

He looked back to her. "But I will give you no names and you will not walk through these streets looking behind doors. If I find someone here is involved in this, we will deal with it our-selves."

Katy said nothing but Louis could tell from the sudden sag of her shoulders that she knew she would get nothing else. She said a brisk goodbye and started back to the Bronco. Louis hurried to catch up with her. Moses Stanton stayed in front of the tribal headquarters doors watching them.

Katy remained silent as she drove around the corner and down a street, pulling up in front of a small stucco house with a concrete porch cluttered with folding chairs. There had once been flowers in the window boxes but they were wilted now, victims of the searing summer sun and neglect.

The front door was open. There were three women on the porch and three men standing in the sparse shade of a tree smoking cigarettes. The women were dressed in cotton blouses and skirts and wore their hair in long braids. The men had lined weathered faces and dusty clothes. But what struck Louis was that another one of his assumptions about Indians was proving wrong. Every man he could see had short hair.

"I won't be long," Katy said, eyeing the women on the porch. "I'll leave the engine going so you can have some air."

"Thanks."

Katy started toward Aunt Betty's house. The few people out-side turned their attention from the SUV to Katy herself. Louis watched closely, curious about the reception she'd get.

Katy paused under the tree and spoke briefly to the men. When they didn't step back to let her on the porch, she steeled herself and slipped between them, disappearing into the house. For a moment, the men looked back at the SUV then went back to talking among themselves.

Louis sank back into the seat. Partly to be less obvious, but mostly because he was groggy. His aching ribs had kept him up most the night and about four in the morning he had finally relented and popped a pain pill. He laid his head against the window and idly watched the parade of people in front of the house.

One woman caught his eye. She wore a bright yellow sun dress and was coming down the street carrying a casserole dish covered with aluminum foil. A second woman followed her, slightly younger, carrying a basket of neatly folded laundry. The men parted to let them inside the house.

Suddenly Louis was somewhere else.

In Bessie's old boarding house in Blackpool, Mississippi. A stranger in his own town of birth, sitting vigil by the bedside of a dying woman he could barely remember — his mother. Women had come then, too. Black women carrying clean linens for his mother and casseroles and cookies for him.

He remembered none of their names but he remembered their voices. Soft and soothing as they gathered by Lila's bed, the sound carrying across the hall to his room where he took refuge when he could.

And then, after Lila died, came the sound of their voices raised joyously in song, drifting up from the room downstairs. He didn't understand why they were happy, these strange women, because his mother had lived a short ugly life, given away her children, given him away, and then she had suffered a painful death. It made him angry to hear their voices.

Bessie had been the one to explain it to him.

Death was a relief from agony. Death was a return to Jesus. Death was a going home.

Louis looked back to the house. The men had wandered off and the porch was empty. There was no one on the street but a couple of kids on bicycles.

Then the house screen door slapped open and two young men exited. One was thin and wore a black t-shirt and jeans. The second was shorter and more tightly muscled, like a football running back. He wore a loose fitting plain white shirt with an odd heavy silver necklace, like a scythe blade on a chain. Both men had long black hair pulled back in pony tails.

The men took a long look at the SUV then lit up cigarettes.

Louis sat up straighter. The stocky kid was still staring his way and Louis knew the kid could see his face behind the glass. The kid tapped the other guy on the shoulder, said something in his ear, and both started away from the house.

Louis got out of the SUV.

The men were heading down the street at a quick clip. Louis had made enough traffic stops and interviewed enough suspects to sense fear. A shift of the body to avoid calling attention to the weight of a gun in a pocket. A twist of the shoulders to release tension. A suddenly quickened pace.

He knew he shouldn't be doing this.

He was nosing around in Katy's territory and she was going to be pissed. But something told him to stay with them, just for a block or two.

At the corner, the thinner guy broke off. The stocky one took one last look back at Louis before turning down a side street.

Louis followed, about thirty feet behind. The guy was walking fast and stiff, his head swiveling back at Louis every few feet. Finally, he reached a yellow house with a yard full of toys and a plastic wading pool. He cut across the grass and quickly slipped inside. Then, despite the heat, he slammed the heavy door.

Louis jogged back to the SUV. Katy was in the driver's seat, both hands resting on the wheel.

As he got in she wiped her face quickly.

"You okay?" he asked.

She shrugged but he could see she was struggling to not cry.

"Where'd you go?" she asked.

"I followed someone," he said. "A guy in his twenties, stocky."

"Why?"

"He was acting hinky."

"Hinky?"

"He went into a yellow house over on the next street."

Katy frowned. "That might be Hachi or one of his friends."

"You know him?"

She shook her head slowly. "Not really."

"He didn't like me following him."

"A black guy gets out of a FWC vehicle and follows you. What young guy here would like that, Louis?"

"Fair enough. But I'm going to run a check on him. What's his last name?"

She hesitated. "Keno."

"Don't worry, I won't get you in trouble with Moses."

She stared at him for a long time then with a final look back at Betty's house, she jammed the SUV into gear and pulled slowly away.

They were out on Alligator Alley heading west into the setting sun before Katy spoke again.

"She's dead," she said softly.

For a second Louis thought she meant her great aunt Betty but then realized she was talking about Grace.

Katy flipped down the visor to retrieve her sunglasses and slipped them on, but not before Louis saw her eyes well with tears.

"You don't know that," Louis said.

She looked left, to the huge empty expanse of the Everglades. "We've increased our search flights, we've got every officer out there looking and all the hunters on alert," she said. "There's no sign of her. She's gone, Louis, Grace is gone."

Maybe it was the emotion of the visit to Betty. Maybe she was just exhausted. But this was the first time he had heard defeat in her voice.

"Look," he said, "Things go cold on cases but then you get a break and things heat up. You have to stay with it, you have to stay positive."

She glanced at him then looked back to the road.

"Go home and try not to worry," he said. "Have a glass of wine and get a good night's sleep. We'll start again early tomorrow."

She was silent.

"You've got to trust me on this," Louis said. "We'll find her, Katy. We'll bring Grace home."

CHAPTER THIRTEEN

For the third time in the last twenty minutes, Louis checked his watch, this time even tapping it to make sure it was running. Almost eight.

Where the hell was Katy?

"Everything okay here?"

He looked up at the waitress. "What? Oh, yeah."

"Top you off?" she asked, holding up the coffee pot.

Louis nodded absently, and she refilled his mug.

Yesterday, after their visit to the reservation, Louis had asked Katy to meet him for breakfast this morning. The forensic report from Grace's crime scene was due back today and he hoped to be able to show it to Katy to boost her mood. When he went to pick it up the tech said he would bring it over to the IHop when he came over to get his takeout coffee.

Louis looked out the window for Katy's FWC Bronco. No sign of it on the morning crawl along Tamiami Trail. He glanced at the pay phone out by the entrance, but he had already called her apartment and gotten the machine. A second call to her office got him a secretary who told him she hadn't come in yet.

The guy from the forensic unit came in the entrance, spotted Louis and came over to his booth.

"Here's your prelim," he said, tossing a manila envelope on the table.

"Thanks," Louis said. "Tell the cashier to add your coffee to my bill."

After the man left, Louis put on his reading glasses and took out the report. He skipped over the tire tread part, focusing in the boot prints that had been found. They were for a men's size ten Timberland Flume, a common hiking boot.

He zeroed in on the cigarette pack. The lab had been able to lift two clean prints from the cellophane but there was no match to anyone in the system.

He turned the page, scanning quickly, then stopped. The techs had found human hairs tangled in some brush. The analysis read: natural black, from the head, straight with circular cross sections, medium-sized pigment granules, and a thicker cuticle, consistent with Mongoloid pattern.

Louis took off his glasses. "Mongoloid" meant someone of Asian or Native-American descent. But he knew this wasn't going to be enough to convince Katy.

He glanced out to the parking lot. Still no sign of her truck. He put his glasses back on and went back to the report.

One hair had its bulb intact, which meant they could test for DNA. But Louis knew there was no point. He had read enough about the new technology to know that a test would take months to come back. Besides, they had no one — and nothing — to compare it to. That wasn't really true, he thought. They had the cigarette butt from the hunting camp but what would that prove? Besides, he had promised Gary Trujillo not to involve him in the case and there was no way Mobley would foot the bill for the high cost of a DNA test.

Louis took a drink of his coffee but it had gone cold.

So would this case if he didn't think of something.

But first he had to find Katy.

He rose, picking up his check. After paying, he called Katy's apartment again. Still no answer. He tried her office, this time getting Jeff, the man who had been with Katy on the call to rescue Bruce from the patio. Jeff remembered Louis and told him that it was unusual for Katy to not check in.

"She's been here every day at the crack of dawn since Grace disappeared," he said. "She's been pulling twelve-hour days and riding us all pretty hard."

"You try to radio her?" Louis asked.

"Yeah, about a half-hour ago. No answer."

"Try again, would you?"

Louis waited, listening while Jeff tried to raise Katy but there was no answer. Jeff came back to the phone.

"She could be out of range if she went out into the Glades," Jeff said.

"Except she was supposed to meet me for breakfast."

"Yeah," Jeff said softly.

"Keep trying the radio," Louis said. "I'll check back in with you in a half hour."

He hung up and looked again to the parking lot. He decided to go to her office. Maybe he and Jeff could go looking for her.

Traffic was bumper-to-bumper on southbound I-75 and the swirl of red and blue lights ahead told Louis there was an accident. He sat, hands tapping on the wheel, gaze wandering out the side window. A sign for the Miromar Outlet Mall caught his eye. He was right near Katy's apartment.

He swung the Mustang onto the shoulder and sped up onto the off-ramp. The apartment complex backed onto the freeway and he found Katy's building and parked. As he was starting toward the stairway he spotted her FWC Bronco sitting in a parking spot.

He breathed out a sigh of relief. Maybe she had taken his advice yesterday to heart and gotten drunk and just slept in.

On the second floor, he knocked on her door. No answer. He pounded harder this time. Nothing. There was a window with closed drapes. He rapped hard on it, hoping it was Katy's bedroom.

The door flew open. A woman poked her head out, her blonde hair wild around her tan face.

"What the hell is it?" she said.

The woman was wearing Joe Boxer pajamas and her face was creased with sleep-lines. Obviously. the roommate.

"Is Katy here?" Louis asked.

"Who are you?"

"Louis. I'm a friend of Katy's and she —"

"She's at work." She started to close the door but Louis wedged a foot in it to stop her.

"Hey!"

"Katy's not at work," Louis said. "You sure she's not here?"

The roommate rubbed her face. "Yeah, I'm sure. I saw her leave early this morning when I got home. I work the night desk at the Clarion and we sort of pass each other coming and going."

"Her car is still in the lot," Louis said.

The woman stepped out and squinted down over the railing. "Huh," she said. "That's weird. She must've taken the Jeep instead."

"What Jeep?"

"Her own car. She keeps it parked in number ten, next to her work truck."

Louis looked down at the FWC Bronco then back at the roommate. "What time did she leave?" he asked.

"About six."

"Was she dressed for work?"

The roommate nodded. "Yeah, the same thing she wears every day, khaki shorts, and one of her ranger shirts over a tee. And that ugly baseball cap."

"Did she take her radio with her?"

"Yeah. She keeps it in a charger on the kitchen counter next to her keys and I saw her take it."

"Does she have a gun?"

"Gun? Yeah, she has a gun."

"Where does she keep it?"

"In her bedside table."

"Would you see if it's there, please?"

The roommate eyed him. "Stay here." She shut the door and locked it. Louis waited, sweat beading on his face. Only nine-fifteen and it was already in the high eighties.

The door jerked open. "The gun's not there," she said, stifling a yawn. "We finished here? I'm pulling an extra shift today and I need my sleep."

Louis thanked the roommate and went back downstairs to the FWC Bronco. It was locked. He looked in the window.

Immaculate as usual. No radio stuck in the console charger. Nothing strange. Except...

There was something on the back seat. He cupped his hands on the back window. Clothing. A white shirt with the prominent FWC emblem on the breast. And Katy's ball cap.

What the hell was going on here?

Louis did a slow scan of the parking lot, his eyes focusing in on the asphalt around the Bronco and its surface. No sign of a struggle.

There was only one explanation. She had started off her day as normal, maybe to meet him for breakfast but had changed her mind. She had left in her personal unmarked car but had apparently felt the need to shed her work shell. There was only one reason she had done it: She had gone back to the reservation and didn't want to be seen as an outsider. But was it on a personal visit to see Aunt Betty? Or was she defying Moses and going to see Keno?

That would explain why she didn't call him. But why hadn't she at least checked in with her office or told them she was going to be late?

He walked back to his Mustang. As he was unlocking the door something in the next car caught the sunlight. He went to the Toyota and peered in the window. It was a piece of silver hanging from the rearview mirror. It was odd-looking, like a woman's heavy silver necklace.

Louis did a quick scan of the Toyota's back seat but saw nothing strange. He went around the back. The plate was from Hendry County, not Lee. The Seminole reservation was located in Hendry.

It meant nothing. But it could mean everything. He jotted down the plate number in his notebook then wiped a sleeve over his sweaty face, pulling in a painful breath.

Something didn't feel right in his gut and it wasn't his bruised ribs.

"You're becoming a pain in the ass, Kincaid."

Louis wasn't in the mood to argue with Mobley but he understood the sheriff's position. The evidence he had offered Mobley about Katy was razor-thin and there was no way the sheriff would authorize a search for someone who had been out of contact for less than four hours.

"I'm late for a meeting," Mobley said.

He picked up a file and headed for the door but then he stopped and looked back. "Are you getting personal with this woman?"

"What?"

"Your Indian lady. Is something going on?"

"Goddamn it, Lance."

Mobley shook his head. "Then why this knee-jerk reaction?"

Louis stared him straight in the eye. "How long you been a cop?"

"Seventeen years."

"Haven't you ever just had a bad feeling about something?"

Mobley's jaw tightened. "What do you want from me?"

"Make a call to the Seminole police. They'll talk to you."

Mobley hesitated then turned to his secretary outside the office. "Ginger, get me the Seminole police chief on the phone."

He went back to his desk and a few seconds later the phone buzzed. Mobley picked up the receiver. Louis waited while Mobley talked to someone he politely addressed as Chief Gilley.

"Ask about Aunt Betty," Louis said.

Mobley covered the receiver. "Who?"

"Katy's aunt. Make sure she didn't die."

Mobley stared at him and went back to his call. A minute later he hung up.

"No one has seen her," he said. "And Aunt Betty is still kicking."

Ginger appeared at the door. "Sheriff, you're really late for your meeting."

"Fuck," Mobley muttered, picking up his file again and headed to the door.

"Sheriff."

Mobley turned with a heavy sigh. "What?"

"Put out an alert on her Jeep," Louis said.

Mobley tapped the folder lightly on his palm, eyeing Louis, before he turned toward his secretary. "Ginger, give him what he needs."

Mobley left. Ginger leaned against the doorframe, giving Louis an appraising glance. "He must really like you," she said.

"No," Louis said. "He likes cats."

Ginger laughed and motioned for Louis to follow her back to her desk. "Give me the info on the alert," she said, sliding a pad toward him. "I'll get it out ASAP."

Louis scribbled Katy's name and a description of her Jeep, knowing Ginger could get the plate number herself.

"This is an attempt to locate," he said, handing her the pad.

"I got it," Ginger said, turning to her computer.

As he watched her, Louis knew this wasn't going to be enough. There was a good chance Katy wasn't even in Lee County right now. Or any place where a cop would spot her Jeep.

He pulled out his notebook. "Run this plate, please."

With a few taps of the keys, a name and address popped onto the computer screen. Louis leaned in to read it – HAYWOOD KENO, 1445 PALMETTO STREET.

Haywood...not Hachi. Unless Hachi was a nickname.

"Ginger, can you pull up this guy's DL?" he asked.

It took a few moments but then the driver's license photo came up. It was the man he had followed yesterday.

Then he remembered the weird silver thing he had seen hanging from the rearview mirror of the Toyota in Katy's parking lot. And he remembered where he had seen one like it before — around Hachi Keno's neck the day he had followed him.

Keno had met Katy in the parking lot and she had left with him. But why? The only explanation was that he convinced her he knew where Grace was. And it wasn't on the reservation — it was somewhere isolated, somewhere no one could hear or see the cat.

Louis stared at the photograph. Keno's eyes stared back, dark and unfathomable. He could read nothing in them. And that bothered him.

"Ginger, I need one more address," Louis said.

CHAPTER FOURTEEN

W hat the hell are you doing here?"

Louis almost hadn't expected to see Gary Trujillo open the door of the neat green-shuttered trailer. With the flower boxes under the windows and the plastic flamingo in the yard he was sure when he drove up that he had the wrong house.

"I need your help," Louis said.

"I told you I don't want to get involved," Gary said, starting to shut the door.

"Katy's missing," Louis said.

"What? What do you mean missing?"

"We were supposed to meet for breakfast and she didn't show. She hasn't been to work or called in. I think she's with a Seminole named Keno and I think he's the guy who took the panther."

Gary came out onto the porch. "You think he took Katy, too?"

"I don't know. She might have gone with him because he told her he knew something about Grace. I don't know. I just know I don't like the feel of it."

"How come you don't just call out the cavalry?"

"The reservation is off limits," Louis said. "But I don't think that's where they are. I think they're out in the Glades somewhere, but Hendry County is out of my jurisdiction. Besides, the cops wouldn't know where to start looking."

Gary was quiet for a moment. "You're thinking he's got this panther hidden somewhere. Somewhere isolated, like a hunting camp."

Louis nodded. "And you know where they all are."

Gary glanced at the sun, which was already starting its slow descent. "I'll go get dressed," he said.

Louis was wearing the same polo shirt and khaki pants he had put on that morning, and now, out here in the sodden-blanket air of the Glades, he was sweat-soaked and mosquito-bitten. It was after five and they were into their second hour of their search.

They had started at Gary's camp, where there had been no sign of any intruders since Louis's encounter there. They had done a quick search of all the "live" camps, but they had all been locked up tight with no signs of intruders. That left the abandoned hunting camps.

"No one knows exactly how many there are," Gary said as they plowed through the brush in his SUV, heading south now. "These camps have been handed down for generations and some families have just given up and left."

One and a half million acres. That was the figure running through Louis's head as he took in the desolate landscape of trees and brush. That was how large the Everglades were. How in the hell were they going to find Katy in all this?

He glanced toward the west. There was only about an hour of daylight left. If they didn't find some trace of Katy or Keno soon they'd have to give up and start again in the morning.

If he could even convince Gary to try again. They had checked out four abandoned camps so far and none had any signs that anyone had been there.

The thick brush parted and Louis spotted a clearing ahead and then a cabin. No, not a cabin, he decided as they drew near, just another listing shack.

There were no fresh tire tracks in the narrow dirt road leading in and no signs of life anywhere in the weed-choked compound. Louis let out a hard breath of disappointment.

"Another dead end," Gary said as steered the SUV in a wide slow circle. "That's it. We're heading back."

"Have we hit them all?" Louis asked.

Gary was quiet, his jaw clenched, eyes trained on the windshield.

"Gary, are there any more camps?"

Gary braked to a hard stop. "Look man, this is nuts. You realize what the chances are of finding anyone out here? Fuck, you're not even sure Katy is really missing."

"I know she is."

"How? You don't even know the woman. You don't know what she's like. She just does this sometimes."

Louis stared at him. "What do you mean?"

Gary's face was red and he was gripping the steering wheel hard. He looked away and shook his head. "Katy and me, we used to be together," he said slowly. "But it got too hard, you know? It was always work with her, always the damn cats. She'd like disappear on me. I wouldn't hear from her for days and then she'd come back saying she was out hunting down a cat or nursing a sick cub or going to some school or to talk to a damn politician."

Katy and Gary? Yeah, it seemed odd. But only on the surface. They both loved the same thing – this awful, desolate, beautiful place.

Gary finally looked at Louis. "I loved her but there was never any room for me. It just got too damn hard."

He looked away, jerking the SUV into gear. They rode in silence for a long time. Louis realized they were not heading west back toward Alligator Alley, that they were still going south. The brush was getting heavier, the terrain changing from prairie to swamp-land.

"I thought we were going back to Fort Myers," Lou-is said.

"There used to be two abandoned camps northwest of Copeland," Gary said. "I don't know if they're still there but we might as well check them out."

Copeland. Louis remembered the place. It was a forlorn little town on the edge of the Fakahatchee Strand Preserve. He and Joe had chased Ben's kidnapper out into the swamp. The man had almost killed Louis before Joe shot him.

Her job had always come first, too. It was why she was now sixteen hundred miles away in Michigan. It was partly why they had split up last Christmas.

He was deep in thought and it took him a moment to realize the SUV had slowed. Gary was leaning forward peering into the thick stand of cypress trees ahead as they inched forward.

"I thought I saw something move," Gary said.

Louis sat up straighter, his eyes straining into the dusk. Then he saw it — a faint quiver of white light. It was there and then it was gone, like a firefly moving through the trees.

"A flashlight?" Louis asked.

Gary braked. "A lantern most likely."

He shut off the engine. The quiet rushed in, followed by the soft sounds of the coming night — frogs and crickets.

"We'd better walk from here," Gary said.

Gary reached in the back and pulled out rifle and a flashlight, sticking the flashlight in his hunter's vest. Louis slid out of the SUV, landing ankle-deep in warm water. He pulled out his Glock and followed Gary.

The outline of a shack materialized out of the gloom. It was constructed of weathered wood with a corrugated metal roof, its two windows boarded up. Louis couldn't see a door; they must have approached from the back. A broken picnic table sat in the high weeds next to two rusted oil drums. In the swampy ground, Louis couldn't make out any tracks. There was no sign of a vehicle, no lights, no sounds. No signs of any life.

"Shit," Gary whispered at his side. "I could have sworn I saw something."

"I saw it, too," Louis said, his Glock trained on the shack's windows. "Let's check the front. You go left, I'll take the right," Louis said.

He crept up to the shack, flattening himself against the wall. He started slowly toward the front of shack.

A sudden *pop!*

He knew that sound. A silencer.

"Fuck! I'm hit!"

Gary. Somewhere to his left in the darkness.

A crashing noise, like someone running through brush.

"Gary!" Louis yelled.

A soft moan. Louis headed toward it.

In the darkness, he almost tripped over Gary's body. Louis dropped to one knee. Gary was lying on his side in the mud, writhing.

"Shit," Gary hissed, gripping his thigh.

"Did you see where he went?"

"No, no, I didn't see anything. Ah, shit, it hurts..."

Suddenly, Gary went limp and quiet.

"Gary! Gary!"

No response. What the hell? Why'd he black out so quickly?

Louis padded Gary's vest and found his flashlight. Crouching low over Gary's body, he switched it on. He had to find the wound, find out how badly Gary was hurt.

No blood. He couldn't even see a hole in his jeans.

Son of a bitch.

Louis switched off the flashlight. It took a moment for his eyes to adjust but finally he could make out the black outline of the far trees. No light. The lantern was gone.

But Louis knew he was out there, waiting. Not with bullets but with tranquilizer darts.

CHAPTER FIFTEEN

The buzzing of insects filled his ears. Sweat burned his eyes.

Damn. He couldn't see a thing.

But he couldn't risk turning on the flashlight and being an easy target for a dart.

Louis pressed his fingers against Gary's neck. His pulse was slow but strong. He remembered that Katy said a tranquilized panther would stay out for at least a half-hour.

He'd have to chance it and leave Gary here.

Louis began to crawl, slowly, silently, alert for every snap of branch or creak of a door opening. When he made it back to the shack, he eased up against the walls, moving back to the shuttered window. He pressed against it, straining to hear anything inside.

Nothing.

Then he heard it...a faint moaning sound.

No, not a moan. A low growl.

Grace was here, inside this shack. But what about Katy? She had to have heard him yell out Gary's name. If she was inside, why hadn't she called out?

Louis slipped around to the front of the shack, feeling his way along the planks for the door, mindful that there might be a cypress stump or porch he could trip over. But there was nothing under his feet but muck.

Grace growled again, louder this time, a deep throated cry that ended in a whimper. It was the strangest sound Louis had ever heard from an animal. Was she dying? Was the bastard performing some sick ritual on her?

Louis drew a breath and held it, hoping to hear a human voice. Nothing.

He knew he had to go in.

But if Grace was loose, wounded and hungry, she might attack him and he might be forced to — God forbid — shoot her. Even if Grace was caged, the shooter could be lying in wait inside and dart him as soon as he opened the door. He would have only a few seconds to return fire. And if he missed, he'd be helpless.

He should retreat. Go back to Gary's SUV and get on the CB radio. Get some help out here, even if it didn't come until dawn. He could keep this shack covered until then.

But then Grace cried again, a pitiful growl that floated in the night a long time before it faded. He couldn't wait. Grace could be dead by morning.

Louis drew up the flashlight and his Glock and stepped to the door. He kicked it in, splintering the jamb.

A scream. Animal scream.

He switched on the flashlight and swung it in an arc. Grace...lying in a cage. Other things registered in a blur. A cot heaped with clothes. A dirty portable toilet. A belt of knives hanging on the wall. And the smell — like rotting meat.

A muffled sound in the dark corner behind him.

He spun.

It was Katy. She was tied up, arms over her head, suspended from a hook on a rafter. In the flashlight beam her eyes were wide and wild above her duct-taped mouth. Her face was streaked with mud and dried blood.

He went to her and peeled off the tape.

She pulled in a ragged breath. "Keno! He's outside!"

"Katy, take a breath."

She was tied with fishing line, looped over the hook. He began to work at the line on her wrists.

"He heard your truck and he tied and gagged me! He took the dart rifle and ran outside. He wants to —"

Something hard came down on the back of Louis's neck. He tumbled forward, almost falling into Katy. He dropped the flashlight and started to grope for it but suddenly he heard Keno working a rifle mechanism. The bastard was trying to load another dart.

Louis scrambled to his feet and suddenly a beam of light beam came up behind him. Katy had worked one hand free and was holding the flashlight. It washed Keno in white light. He stood, holding the large sighted rifle. His hands were shaking, his clothes were caked with mud and his face was dripping with sweat.

"Freeze!" Louis shouted, leveling the Glock at him.

"No. No, you don't understand," Keno said.

"Drop the damn gun!"

"I need to do this," Keno said. "I need to save her. I need to save her now."

"Drop the fucking gun!"

"Louis!" Katy said. "Don't shoot him. He's —"

Keno got the dart chambered.

Damn it! He didn't want to shoot this guy, not in front of Katy but the bastard wasn't leaving him any choice.

"Louis, he's trying to save Aunt Betty!" Katy cried. "He thought the panthers would —"

Keno started to raise the rifle.

Louis fired.

The bullet caught Keno in the shoulder and spun him around. Keno dropped the rifle and fell, landing half outside the door.

Katy let out a strangled cry. Louis went to Keno and snatched up the rifle. He had aimed only to wound, hitting Keno in the shoulder. It was enough to bring him down but he wasn't going to die.

A howl. Deep and pained, coming from Grace.

"Louis! Untie me! Quick!" Katy yelled.

He started back to Katy but saw the belt hanging on the wall and grabbed one of the knives. He had barely sliced through the fishing line before Katy yanked away and ran to the cage.

Louis used a piece of the fishing line to tie Keno to the door latch. Keno looked up at him then hung his head.

"Louis!"

He turned to Katy. She was crouched next to the cage, holding the flashlight on Grace. He got his first good look at the panther.

She was sprawled on her side in the small cage, all four legs out, her body heaving with labored breaths. The cage was littered with feces, small bones and uneaten food of some kind. Grace's coat was matted with brown mud.

He went to Katy's side.

"How did you find me?" Katy asked.

"I got worried and hunted down Gary,' Louis said. "We checked all the abandoned camps."

She looked at him, her face half-lit in the light. "Gary? Where is he?"

"Keno got him with the dart," Louis said. "He's outside, twenty, thirty feet from the shack."

Katy nodded, her face slick with sweat. "Get me Keno's rifle."

"What?"

"Just get it!"

Louis got the rifle and brought it to Katy. When she stood up, she wavered. Louis held out a hand but she brushed it away and took the rifle.

Grace let out a bellow filled with pain.

"Take this and hold it so I can see her," she said. Her hand was shaking as she gave him the flashlight.

Louis took the flashlight and trained it on the panther. Katy took two steps back. Her eyes were filled with tears. She raised the rifle.

"Katy, wait! Don't! We can take her — "

"She's in pain, damn it!"

Grace raised her head, her eyes coming up to Katy.

Katy fired.

A sharp *pop!*

Grace's head fell hard and her yellow eyes went blank.

CHAPTER SIXTEEN

Louis stared at the motionless panther. He didn't even realize Katy had moved away until he felt something brush his shoulder. She was holding a blanket.

"I need your help," she said.

"What?"

"There's a Coleman lantern in here somewhere. Find it and bring it over to the cage."

"Katy —"

"Just do it, please!"

She knelt and untied the wire on the cage door. Louis swung the flashlight around the room until he found the lantern and some matches. He lit the lantern and brought it to Katy.

In the hard light of the lantern he got a better look at Grace. What he had thought was brown mud was dried blood, concentrated around her haunches. There was a small pool of fresh pink blood near her tail.

Katy swung the cage door open and ducked inside, grabbing Grace's front legs.

"Help me get her out onto the blanket," Katy said. "Take her back legs but be gentle."

"Katy, what are you doing?"

"We have to get her out of the cage so we have room to work."

"Work?"

Katy looked up at Louis, her eyes bright with a mixture of fear and — good god — excitement.

"Grace is in labor," she said.

Louis glanced back at Grace. Now he could see the bulge in her belly. And labor explained the fresh blood.

Katy was examining the panther, pressing on her abdomen. "She's too weak to do this herself," she said. "We need to help her. There's only one kitten."

Louis's mind started spinning with options. Move the truck up closer and load Grace in, use the CB to call for a chopper or something.

"Katy, we can get someone here in an hour," he said.

Her head shot up. "No!" she said. "We can't wait. I don't know what the tranquilizer will do to the fetus. Grace and the kitten could be dead in an hour."

Katy looked back to the panther. "The amniotic sac is visible but Grace can't push it out." She shook her head. "Damn, I don't have gloves or antiseptic, I don't have any oxytocin. damn it..."

Louis knelt, setting the lantern on the wood floor. "All right," he said. "What do you need me to do?"

Katy gave him a wavering smile. "Bring me the knife and see if you can find a clean towel or something. And I need a piece of that fishing line."

Louis rose and used the flashlight to do a quick scan of the shack. The place was decrepit and filthy, with nothing but some fast food wrappers and some jugs of bottled water. He finally found Keno's knap-sack. It held some toiletries and some men's underwear.

He cut off some fishing line and took it and a pair of blue boxer shorts to Katy. She didn't even look up as she took them.

"Hang on, Grace," Katy whispered.

Louis could see a small greenish sac protruding from beneath Grace's tail. He shut his eyes. A weird memory flashed to his brain, that day back in the police academy when they had breezed through the part in the textbook about delivering babies.

When he opened his eyes, Katy was carefully pulling out the sac. He watched, fascinated, as she wrapped the kitten in the blue shorts and broke the sac. She severed the cord with the knife and used an edge of the shorts to clean the fluid and tissue from the kitten's mouth and nose.

"You need to tie the cord," she said, nodding to the piece of fishing line.

"What?"

"Cut off a small piece of the line and tie it, close to the kitten's belly."

Louis knelt, sliced off a piece of line and carefully tied the umbilical cord. He sat back on his haunches, watching the kitten.

"It's not breathing," he said.

"I know," Katy said. She began to rub the kitten briskly with the shorts. She rose suddenly, still cradling it. "There's water somewhere in here. Where it is?"

"Over there," Louis said, pointing.

Katy disappeared. Louis stayed crouched by the Grace, watching her closely. She was still out, but her lower abdomen was moving.

Suddenly, a second green blob appeared.

"Katy!"

"What?"

"There's another one coming."

"What? I only felt one!"

Louis could see the kitten's head protruding now. But nothing else was happening.

"It's stuck," he yelled.

"You'll have to pull it out."

He yanked off his polo shirt and scooted closer to Grace. He wrapped the edge of the shirt over the kitten's head and pulled downward gently but firmly.

Come on...

Slowly, the slimy little creature emerged. He grabbed the knife from the floor, carefully cut through the umbilical cord and tied it off.

Then he let out a breath, sat back on his haunches and looked down at the kitten cradled in his shirt. It was wiggling but its face was covered with tissue.

Gently, he rubbed the kitten's nose and mouth like he had seen Katy do. At first the kitten didn't respond then it opened its tiny mouth and let out a noise like a rusty hinge.

Yes. Breathe. That's right. Breathe.

Another weak mew and the kitten settled in the folds of the shirt in Louis's hands. He supposed he should set it down next to Grace, but he wanted to hold it just a moment longer.

"Congratulations, dad."

Louis looked up over his shoulder at Katy. Her face was slick with sweat and dirt. She looked exhausted but she was smiling.

"I'm glad you find this funny," he said. He looked at the blood on her hands.

"Did the other one make it?" he asked.

She nodded.

Louis looked at Grace. The panther's head was still down but her eyes were open now and her chest rose and fell in an even rhythm.

"Is Grace going to be okay?" Louis asked.

"Yes, she'll be fine," Katy said. She looked toward Keno, slumped near the door.

"What about Hachi?

"He'll make it," Louis said.

There was a sudden shuffling sound outside. Louis tensed and started to look for a spot to set his kitten down but then a bulky familiar frame filled the door-way.

Gary stood there, hands braced on the frame, wavering. His eyes went from Keno lying at his feet to Grace and finally back to Louis.

"What the fuck happened?" he asked.

Louis held up the kitten. "Congratulations," he said. "You're an uncle."

CHAPTER SEVENTEEN

What the fuck happened here?"

The man standing in front of Louis — Hendry County sheriff Amos Zeedler — was sweaty, sleepy and confused. It was dawn and he had just arrived at the shack in a muddy white SUV, trailed by two detectives in a county swamp buggy. One of the detectives stood in the open-air buggy holding his rifle and looking like an anxious Secret Service agent on a rooftop. The other was hovering around Gary's SUV, making small talk.

The Hendry entourage had been led here by Gary who had reluctantly left late last night to summon help once it had been decided that four humans and a cage holding a panther would not fit in Gary's truck. And Katy's Jeep was too low on gas to travel far.

"I asked what the fuck happened?" Zeedler asked again, looking hard at Louis. "Who's been kidnapped? Who's been shot? Who shot him and who the hell are you?"

"Louis Kindcaid," Louis said, producing the badge Mobley had given him. Zeedler's dark eyes flicked to the badge and back to Louis's face. He seemed surprised there was a cop on the scene.

Louis had asked Gary to tell the Hendry County sheriff that a Lee County officer was involved and that Mobley would need to be notified. Apparently Gary had forgotten that last part.

"You're one of Mobley's guys," Zeedler muttered.

Louis ignored the slight. "Yes, sir. Could you tell me if you have notified Sheriff Mob —"

"Who got shot here?" Zeedler's eyes shot up to Louis, squinting against the rising sun.

"An Indian named Hachi Keno."

"Is Keno alive?"

"Yes, sir. He's tied up inside."

"Was he armed?" Zeedler asked.

"Yes, he had —"

"Fuck," Zeedler muttered again, looking off toward the cypress trees. "An officer-involved shooting. Just what I need right now."

"With all due respect, sir, I'm not your officer and most of the paperwork and investigation will fall to Lee County."

Zeedler looked back at him. "Who did this Keno guy kidnap?"

Louis was sure the sheriff wouldn't notify Mobley until he knew exactly what had happened and how it would play out in the media.

Damn Gary.

He had done a piss-poor job at explaining things to Zeedler. And Louis knew why. Gary had hoped to give them enough information to get Hendry County out here, and then he planned to turn into a ghost, just like he had after the episode with the Fort Lauderdale robbers. But that wasn't going to happen this time. The Hendry County deputy had not left the side of Gary's SUV.

"The victim, officer," Zeedler repeated. "Who did Keno kidnap?"

"Her name is Katy Letka," Louis said. "She's an officer with the Florida Wildlife Commission."

"And that Gary guy outside, how is he involved in all this?"

"Katy and I were working on a poaching case. When Katy disappeared yesterday morning, I suspected Hachi Keno had taken her and was keeping her at one of these old camps. Gary knew about the camps and we spent most yesterday searching. We found her and Keno last night."

Zeedler blew out a breath and again wiped his brow. He was so sweaty his dark uniform looked as if were melting onto his body.

"Don't fuck around with me, officer," Zeedler said. "You're a cop. Why not just arrest Keno last night and drive him and the victim back into town in Gary Toot-whatever's vehicle?"

Louis hadn't been fucking with Zeedler but he would now.

"Because we couldn't have brought Grace with us."

Zeedler yanked off his hat. "Who the fuck is Grace?"

"Follow me," Louis said.

"Now wait a minute," Zeedler said.

Louis walked toward the shack. "Follow me, sir."

Zeedler hesitated then decided to follow Louis to the shack. When Louis pushed open the door and Zeedler stepped inside, his hand went immediately to cover his nose.

Louis had heard that sunshine was the best disinfectant but in this case, the light only elevated the place from disgusting to revolting. Feces. Bones. Maggots. Rust.

How Katy had stayed in here all night, Louis didn't know. It had to be a powerful devotion to Grace and those kittens. Even now, she was still sitting on the floor near the cage. He could tell she was exhausted but her eyes were lit with exhilaration.

Keno was tied to a hook on the opposite side of the shack, awake but pale. Katy had taken off his shirt and cleaned his wound the best she could. Louis's bullet had caught him in the fleshy part of his shoulder, exiting cleanly. But even a minor gun wound could easily become infected.

"Sheriff Zeedler," Louis said. "That's officer Katy Letka, on the floor."

Katy raised a hand in a weary acknowledgement.

"That man is Hachi Keno," Louis said, "and that's Grace in the cage."

Zeedler spun back to Louis. "Grace is a goddamn panther?" he asked.

"Yes, sir."

"You son of a bitch," Zeedler said. "You sneak into my jurisdiction, you solicit civilian help in a search for a kidnapper and then you shoot an Indian — all over a goddamn lost panther?"

"Poached panther," Louis corrected. "Keno abducted Grace, which is what started all this."

Zeedler just stood there, hand back at his mouth, his gaze circling the tiny shack. He was blanching a little and Louis hoped he would at least move outside if he puked up his coffee.

"Now will you call my sheriff and get him out here?" Louis asked.

Zeedler lowered his hand. His eyes grew even smaller, like shiny drops of oil. "Yeah, I'll call your sheriff. And I'll be surprised if you even have a job when he gets a load of all this crap."

Louis suspected Zeedler was probably right, but he said nothing.

Zeedler grabbed his radio and told his dispatcher to contact Sheriff Mobley. He added that he would be transporting a suspect to the hospital. Then he jammed the radio back in his belt and pointed to Keno.

"Untie that man," Zeedler said. "I'm arresting him for kidnapping."

"There was no kidnapping," Katy said. "I went with him willingly."

Louis glanced at Katy, not surprised she didn't want Keno arrested. During the long night, Louis had wandered in and out of the hot fetid shack but Katy had stayed inside, watching Grace and the kittens but also talking to Keno. Even standing outside, Louis could hear the soft murmur of their voices. Keno would clam up every time Louis came back inside. Louis didn't know exactly what Keno had told Katy but he had the feeling they had reached some understanding about Grace and some forgiveness about what Keno had done to Katy.

Zeedler stared at Katy for a moment then looked back to Keno, who was now paying attention to what was happening. He looked terrified.

"Then I'm taking him in for poaching an endangered animal," Zeedler said.

A new voice came from behind them, deep and commanding. "I don't think so."

Everyone turned to the doorway. Moses Stanton stood there, arms crossed.

Like Zeedler had done, Moses took in the interior of the shack, his eyes resting a long time on Katy and Grace. He stepped inside and slowly took off his hat.

"Who the fuck are you?" Zeedler asked.

"Moses Stanton, executive assistant to the Seminole chief."

"And who the hell called you?" Zeedler asked.

"Smoke signals," Moses said, with a small smile.

"Very funny, Stanton," Zeedler said.

"Let's get to the point," Moses said. "You have no reason to be here, sheriff."

"The hell I don't. We're in my county," Zeedler said. "And that panther over there is a federally protected animal. That means no one can hunt it. Not even Indians."

"You're wrong, sheriff," Moses said. "May I remind you of a 1985 case right here in Hendry County. A Seminole man killed a panther and the state charged him with a felony for killing an endangered animal."

"I remember that," Zeedler said. "He got off because the court ruled old treaties said you could hunt what you wanted on the reservation. But this panther is not on your land."

"The lawyers said the treaties gave us the right to hunt anywhere, not just on our own land," Moses said. "And it was argued that the Seminole had the right to kill the panther to use in a religious ritual."

Louis glanced at Katy. She gave him a small shake of her head as if to warn him not to ask any questions.

"It doesn't matter what the fucking lawyers said," Zeedler said. "The case was dismissed."

Moses nodded. "Do you want to spend the next two years fighting about this again?"

For a moment, Zeedler looked so angry he couldn't draw a breath. But then the anger faded to simple frustration. He looked down at Keno and then at Grace in the cage.

He shook his head. "All right," he said. "I'm not going to the mat over a fucking cat." He looked at Louis. "Mobley can deal with this — and you."

Zeedler pushed by Moses out the door. Louis turned to watch him as he stalked back through the tall grass toward his swamp buggy.

"I will be taking Hachi with me," Moses said.

"I can't let you do that," Louis said.

"Why not?"

"Because I shot him," Louis said.

Moses nodded. "He probably deserved it," he said.

"That's not the point," Louis said. He wiped his sweating forehead, his head clouded from exhaustion. "I'm a cop," he said. "I'm looking at a shit storm because of this."

Moses smiled slightly. Then he turned to Katy.

"Did Hachi hurt you?" he asked.

"He didn't mean to," Katy said.

"Did he hurt the panther?"

"He didn't know how to help her. That's why he brought me here."

Moses went to Keno and knelt by his side. He carefully removed the cloth Katy had put on Keno's bare shoulder and examined the wound. Then he tilted Keno forward and looked at his back.

"It doesn't look bad," he said, looking up at Louis. "The bullet went right through."

Moses rose and began to search for something, running his hand along the wood planks near the door. Louis realized he was looking for the bullet.

"It's to your left," Louis said.

Moses pulled out a pocket knife.

"Leave it there," Louis said.

Moses popped the bullet out of the wood.

"You just contaminated the crime scene," Louis said.

Moses looked at him. "There was a crime committed here?"

"There was a shooting, damn it!"

Moses gave him a small smile then put the bullet in his mouth and swallowed it.

"What shooting?" Moses said.

Louis stared at him, stunned.

Zeedler was back. He thrust a radio at Louis's chest. "Mobley wants to talk to you. You're on a secure channel."

Moses slipped out of the shack. Louis stood in the doorway watching him.

"Kincaid! You there?"

Louis keyed the radio. "Yeah...yeah, I'm here."

"Sheriff Zeedler tells me you've got a mess out there. You shot the suspect?"

Louis rubbed his face. "Yes, sir. He's okay."

The radio was silent and Louis knew Mobley was thinking that this was going to be shit storm for him, too.

"You stay put," Mobley said finally. "I'll call the reservation and talk to Chief Gilley. Maybe I can save your ass."

Louis looked outside at Moses. He was just standing there, smoking a cigarette and looking up at the sky.

"I don't think you'll need to, sheriff," Louis said. "I don't think the tribe is interested in prosecuting me. I think they consider this a family thing."

"You telling me they don't care you shot one of them?"

"That's exactly what I'm telling you, sir."

Mobley was quiet for a second, then asked, "How's the woman?"

Katy was still sitting on the floor by the cage. Her head was down on her knees.

"Katy's fine. But I need to get her out of here."

"And the cat?"

Louis moved over to the cage. Grace seemed to be sleeping. One of the kittens had crawled away. It was the one Louis had delivered. He could tell because it had more spots than the other one. It raised its tiny head and looked up, its eyes as blue as the sky. He wanted to think the kitten was looking at him but he knew it was probably only attracted to the sunlight coming from the door.

"The cat is fine, sir," Louis said. "So are her kittens."

"Kittens?"

"Yes, sir."

There was a long silence.

"They have blue eyes," Louis said. "They'll photograph well."

There was no response and Louis thought Mobley had just clicked off, probably satisfied that he wasn't going to have to wade through the jurisdictional swamp of the Seminole sovereign nation thing over one of his deputies. No, not even a real deputy. A private eye he had semi-hired during an alcoholic haze and sent him on a joke of a case so he could justify not giving him a real chance to wear a badge.

There was a huge spider web in the corner of the open door. Louis stared at it, watching the yellow and black spider move slowly toward a squirming exhausted fly. A burst of radio from the radio brought him back.

"You still there, Kincaid?"

"Yeah, I'm still here."

"Well done, deputy Kincaid," Mobley said. "Well done."

CHAPTER EIGHTEEN

It was too hot to eat. It was too hot to sleep. It was too hot to even move.

Louis lay still on his bed amid the damp tangled sheets, staring up at the ceiling fan. It did almost nothing to cool the cottage down but it was all he had now. Yesterday the air conditioner had finally died and his weasel landlord Pierre said it would be at least three days before he could get a new unit installed.

Louis looked down at the foot of the bed. Issy was sprawled on her side, all four legs extended, unmoving. He rose on one elbow to watch her. It took a minute but he finally saw the gentle rise and fall of her thin chest.

It was almost too hot to even breathe.

He rose, pulled on a pair of shorts and went out into the living room, glancing at the stove clock. Almost five. He had napped for two hours.

Louis grabbed a Heineken and started toward the porch, stopping as his eyes fell on the telephone and the answering machine. The machine's steady red light stared back at him like a taunting eye.

He had called Lily this morning but there had been no answer and he had to assume — hope — that Lily and her mother were still away at ballet camp. He still hadn't told her he wasn't going to make it up to Michigan in time for her birthday but he was determined not to break the news with a message.

Louis took a swig of beer. He had called Joe, too. No answer at her cabin and he hadn't had to guts the call her office, afraid he'd be told she was still on vacation.

He took another long drink of beer. He didn't want to think of her, lying in some big bed at the Ritz Carlton in Montreal with some guy.

He brought the cold beer bottle up to his sweating forehead and closed his eyes.

Screw this.

He grabbed a second beer and went out onto the porch. The sea oats on the low dune beyond his yard were swaying slightly. If there was any air to be found, it would be down by the water.

The beach was deserted. No one searching for shells, no one braving the bite of no-see-ums. Late August on Captiva. Even paradise could sometimes feel like hell.

Louis dropped down onto the beach, wedged the unopened beer in the sand and took a drink from the open one. As he watched the sun's slow descent into the gulf, he tried to will his mind to go blank. But Joe was there at his side.

Have you ever heard of the green flash?

No, Louis, but I suspect you're going to tell me about it.

It's an atmospheric phenomenon where if conditions are just right, the top of the sun will turn green just before it disappears. The Celts believed that anyone who sees it can never be hurt by love.

He had shut his eyes, giving in to the lull of the surf and he didn't hear her come up behind him.

"Hey there, stranger."

He looked up into Katy's face.

"I followed your footprints down here," she said.

He smiled and patted the sand. "Have a seat."

She sat down, cross-legged on the sand next to him. "Where have you been? I called you a couple days ago."

"I had to go down to Bonita Springs for a deposition. I'm testifying in an insurance fraud trial next month."

"I tried the sheriff's office, too, but they said they hadn't seen you around." She paused. "So the job there didn't work out after all?"

He took a long draw from the beer. "Haven't heard," he said.

Katy was quiet for a moment. "You see that picture of Mobley in the paper?"

Louis nodded. "Yeah. He was holding my kitten."

"How do you know it was yours?"

"I just did."

She chuckled. "I named it Lou."

Louis turned to her. "Lou?"

She shrugged. "The only rocker I could think of was Lou Reed. The other kitten is named Nico, after his girlfriend."

"Lou...close enough." He held out the second beer. "You want one?"

She nodded, took the bottle and popped the top. After taking a drink she set it down in the sand front of her. "I called you because I wanted to explain about Hachi."

Louis knew that Mobley had reached a détente with the Seminole police chief and Keno had gone back to the reservation. No charges had been filed by anyone or against anyone.

"I know it bothers you that he got away with it," Katy said. "But you need to understand why he did it."

"Katy —"

She held up a hand. "I want to tell you." She pulled in a deep breath. "I left the rez when I was twenty so I didn't know much about him but Moses told me what I am telling you. Hachi's mother died when he was very young and in the tribe your social place is counted only through your mother's side. He was taken in by my great aunt Betty's family even though she is of a different clan. Hachi was a lonely kid. Even after the ceremony —"

She stopped to look at Louis. "The Seminoles have a special ceremony to recognize a boy's entrance to manhood. Even after that, he couldn't seem to find his place. He didn't really belong to anyone or anything."

"Lots of people don't fit in," Louis said. "But they don't commit crimes."

"But in his mind it wasn't a crime."

"So why'd he go after the panthers?"

Katy let out a sigh. "It's complicated. The tribe has doctors but they also still have shamans."

"What, like medicine men?" Louis asked.

She nodded. "They use plants and animal parts to treat our people. They are important in our ceremonies and are very respected in the tribe. Hachi wanted to go to medical school but didn't even make it through high school so he decided he was going to become a medicine man."

"You just become a medicine man?"

"No, and that was the problem. Shamans are chosen and trained from boyhood."

Louis was quiet, watching the sunset. "You said something back at the shack about Keno wanting to use the panther to help your aunt. Is that what this was all about?"

"Yes," Katy said quietly. "He believed that if he could get the placenta of a mother panther he could use it to cure Aunt Betty's sickness. That's why he tried to take Bruce, to mate with Grace. But then he realized Grace was already pregnant. And he came to get me to help."

Louis shook his head. "I have to ask, Katy. Is he mentally ill?"

She sighed. "No, just lost. And desperate to help Aunt Betty, to stop something no one can stop."

They fell silent. The sun was hovering just above the horizon as the sky began its slow kaleidoscopic color shift.

Katy leaned forward, drawing her finger through the sand to make two intersecting lines.

"What's that?" Louis asked.

"The world," she said.

"I thought the world was round?"

"This is the world of man's two souls."

"I thought we only had one."

In the waning light he saw her smile. "Humor me," she said.

"Okay, go ahead."

"The Seminoles believe we all have two souls," she said. "The first one is the one that leaves our bodies when we die. The second one, the ghost soul, leaves the body when we dream and it sort of just wanders around until we wake up."

"I've had nights like that," Louis said.

"Well, our dream soul needs to travel to the north, but sometimes it gets lost and goes across the s so-lo-pi he-ni. That's our word for the Milky Way, the road that leads to the west. The west is where the dead souls go. If a ghost soul wanders into the west then when the person wakes up their ghost soul is forever sick."

She brushed the sand from her hands. "That's what happened to Hachi."

Louis was staring down at the lines in the sand. "Do we all go north in our dreams?"

She looked over at him and smiled. "Yes. The north is the place of happiness."

Louis was quiet. A sudden breeze blew in from the water, cool and smelling of rain. Far out over the gulf, a zigzag of lightning lit up the purple clouds then it was dark again.

"It's getting late," Katy said. "I better go."

"Want to go get a burger or something?" Louis asked.

"I can't. I'm going over to see my aunt. And I want to talk to Moses about working part time on the reservation."

"Really? Doing what?"

"They can use a good vet." She paused. "I want to get back inside. You know what I mean?"

"Yeah," Louis said. "Yeah, I do."

CHAPTER NINETEEN

Louis stopped at the glass doors to the county building and squinted at his reflection.

Not bad for an off-the-rack Dillard's clearance suit. It fit him perfectly, but it was so cheap and stiff it make a sound like cellophane if he bent his arms. But he had hit for a Ferragamo blue tie and crisp white shirt. He looked like he could be going to a job interview or a funeral.

He wished he knew which one it was going to be.

Louis yanked open the door and was met inside by icy air and a cacophony of voices. Suits and deputies were everywhere and radio traffic echoed through the tiled halls.

It had been almost a week since he had found Grace. Mobley had finally called him at seven this morning, waking Louis from a sound sleep.

He expected Mobley would grudgingly concede the job, saying something like "It's a done deal. Come in later to start your paperwork."

But he hadn't said that. He said something else.

We need to talk. My office. Two sharp.

Louis had crawled out of bed and sat there for a minute, his hopes slowly dying as he started to question the reasons for Mobley's terse phone call.

There was a chance Mobley was just screwing with him again. Making him wait, making him hold his breath. Mobley had already said he had done a good job, and the sheriff's photo with the kittens had been picked up by newspapers as far away as Arizona. How could Mobley not give him this job?

But it might not be completely up to Mobley. Maybe there were other hoops to jump through, other people Louis had to face. The undersheriff. The lawyers handling the EEOC lawsuits Mobley was facing. Maybe even the county board of supervisors who probably weren't too eager to let Mobley hire a PI whose face had been on the cover of *Criminal Pursuits* magazine.

Which is why Louis had gone to Dillard's this morning and bought the suit he couldn't afford and shined his only pair of dress shoes with a banana peel, a trick he had learned in the academy.

If he was going to stand up before a firing squad at least he'd look good.

Mobley's reception area was empty. Ginger's desk looked abandoned. Photos, the pink ceramic pen holder and the plants on her credenza were gone. So was her nameplate.

The office door opened and Mobley came out. His eyes swept over Louis. "Nice threads. What happened to your old blazer?" he asked.

"Don't ask."

Mobley didn't smile but his eyes showed a hint of amusement as he led Louis into the office. It was ice cold, the force of the air conditioner rattling the closed blinds. Mobley's desk was stacked with folders and papers. His inbox had overflowed into the empty out-box. The trashcan was stuffed. A pile of newspapers covered his back shelf.

"Sorry for the mess," Mobley said. "I'm short-handed."

"Where's Ginger?" Louis asked.

"She got promoted."

"To what?"

Mobley had to think for a minute. "Executive Director of Compliance for Fair and Equal Employment Opportunities in Law Enforcement Environments."

"Sounds like a lawyer's job."

"She is a lawyer," Mobley said. "Passed the bar last month."

Louis had always assumed Ginger was another of Mobley's empty-headed bimbos. He did that too often, he realized, assuming things. He had made assumptions about Katy, about Indians, about hunters and even about panthers. None proved accurate.

"Sit down, Kincaid."

"I'll stand, if you don't mind."

Mobley picked up a folder. "This is what took me so long to get back to you," he said. "It's the results of your background check."

Louis said nothing.

"I suppose I should have made my original offer contingent on a background check since no matter how much I might want to hire someone, some things in a man's past are automatic eliminators that I can do nothing about."

Louis stiffened his spine, trying not to show his disappointment.

"I don't particularly like some of the things you did when you were in uniform in Michigan," Mobley said. "And I don't like how you've handled some of your cases here in Florida. Or the large number of shitheads you've had to shoot."

Louis stayed quiet, fighting the urge to just thank Mobley for the chance at wearing a badge and get the hell out of here.

"But," Mobley went on, "no matter your methods, you're an honest man. Your moral compass, to coin a phrase, is pointed in the right direction."

He had it. He had the job.

"I can teach a man a lot of things," Mobley said. "I can't teach integrity. I want to hire you."

"Thank —" Louis cleared his throat. "Thank you, sir."

"It's only as a deputy," Mobley said.

"I'm fine with that."

"But..."

Mobley's face went wobbly. For a second, Louis thought the man was going to cry. But then, with a kick to the heart, he realized he was smiling. No, not quite. Just trying his damnedest not to smile.

This is going to be a really big but.

"The county's just announced a hiring freeze," Mobley said.

Louis could feel himself shrinking, like the cheap suit was the only thing holding him up.

"I can't take you on right now," Mobley said.

"Then when?" Louis said sharply.

"Things will ease up after the first of the year," Mobley said. "Maybe."

Four months...

Could he take this man's word for it? He would have to. There was nothing else out there. There was no other person who would give him another chance to wear a badge.

Four months...

Of what? Working out in gyms until he couldn't make a fist? Enduring the curious stares of the cops at the tactical gun range? Reading statute books until he went blind?

Four months of living on hope.

"Look, Kincaid, you know you have to recertify to work in Florida anyway," Mobley said. "The next course starts January 15. The rest is up to you."

Louis gave him a tight nod.

Mobley was quiet for a moment as the air conditioner rattled the blinds behind him. He rose.

"You're a pain in the ass, Kincaid," he said. "But I still want you to be *my* pain in the ass. We clear?"

Mobley stuck out his hand. Louis hesitated then came forward and shook his hand.

"Yes, sir, we're clear," Louis said.

Mobley motioned to the door. "Now get the hell out of here. I have the final interviews for Ginger's job."

Mobley opened the door. Three striking young women in business suits, sitting in chairs along the wall, looked up.

The first had flowing dark brown hair, large brown eyes and long shapely legs crossed at the knees. Hispanic.

The second woman wore her black hair sleekly pulled back, set off with gold hoop earrings and red lipstick. African- American.

The third woman was petite, with silky black hair cut around her face in a swish-swish style that made her look younger than she probably was. She wore no make-up but she didn't need any. Her skin was smooth as porcelain. Asian.

Louis looked back to Mobley and raised a brow. "Interesting group of candidates," he whispered.

"Yeah," Mobley said. "Diversity is a beautiful thing."

CHAPTER TWENTY

O utside, Louis paused at the Mustang to yank off his tie and shuck the stiff suit jacket. He tossed them into the backseat.

Hell, he had waited five years to get his badge back. He could wait four more months. This wasn't the slam dunk he had wanted, but it was still good enough. He wanted to share this moment with someone.

Mel. But then he remembered that he had gone to Atlanta with his girlfriend Yuba to meet her mother.

Susan Outlaw and her son Ben. But they wouldn't really understand how important this was.

Sam Dodie. His old chief from Mississippi would get it but Sam and Margaret were roaming around out west somewhere in their motor home.

Phillip. But his foster father was thirteen-hundred miles away up in Michigan and this wasn't something that could be celebrated over the phone.

Joe...

More than anyone she would know what this meant to him. But he wasn't ready to talk to her yet, wasn't ready to find out if her trip to Montreal had been her way of moving on after their argument last Christmas.

Louis looked over the hood of the car toward the station, watching as two cops come out in street clothes, laughing as they headed toward their cars, probably bound for O'Sullivan's. For a second, he considered going there but he decided to wait until he had a badge.

He got in the Mustang, started it up and turned the air on high. For a moment he just sat there, hands on the wheel, squinting out the windshield into the low-slung white sun.

Katy.

Katy would get it.

He glanced at his watch. She'd still be at her office for at least another hour. He slammed the Mustang in gear and peeled out of the lot.

Her desk was empty but there was a full cup of steaming coffee sitting amid the mess of papers. There was no one else in the office, so Louis headed back toward the area holding the panther cages.

There was Katy, standing behind a metal table holding a plastic baby bottle. Jeff was beside her, a wadded up towel in his hands.

"Louis!" Katy said, looking up.

"Hey Katy," he said. "How's it going, Jeff?"

"Fine, Mr. Kincaid."

"Louis, it's Louis, okay?" As he came forward he realized Jeff was cradling a panther kitten in the towel. It was squirming and making raspy mewing noises.

"Oh man," Louis said. "Is that Lou?"

"Yup," Katy said.

"He's gotten big in a week."

Katy nodded. "He's going to be a really big boy, maybe over one-forty." She held up the bottle. "Hold him tight, Jeff. Let's give him the rest of his vitamins."

The kitten was fighting to get out of the towel but Jeff firmly wrapped its legs and Katy injected the last of the white liquid into the tiny pink mouth.

Louis heard a huffing noise and looked to the cage at his left. Grace was pacing, watching them anxiously. The second kitten, Nico, was asleep in the back of the cage.

"Okay, we're done," Katy said.

Louis watched as Jeff opened a small door of the cage and carefully set the kitten back inside. Grace immediately began licking it. After a moment, she grabbed it by the nape and took it back to the corner.

Louis watched them, thinking about the signs he had seen coming onto the preserve and across Alligator Alley. PANTHER CROSSING. DRIVE CAREFULLY.

"How long will you keep them here?" he asked.

"A couple more weeks," Katy said. "Then we have to release them."

Louis turned to look at her. He was puzzled that he didn't see any sadness in her expression. But then he realized that any sentimentality he might have about the cats wasn't part of Katy's makeup. She could love the cats but she couldn't let herself get too attached. It was like his job in a strange way. He could care about the people he helped, fight for the victims, and even mourn the dead. But if he let any of it sit in his heart too long he couldn't do what he needed to do.

Jeff called out a goodbye and left, heading out a back door.

Katy glanced over Louis, taking in his dress slacks and shirt for the first time. "Hot date?" she asked.

"No, job interview. I'm going back in uniform."

Her smile widened. "That's great. I know how much you wanted it."

"That's why I'm here," he said. "Want to go have a beer to help me celebrate?"

She shook her head. "I'd love to, Louis, but I can't right now. Jeff and I have to —"

Louis held up a hand. "Work. I get it. Some other time maybe."

She cocked her head. "You want to come help us?"

"Help you do what?"

"We're releasing Bruce today. Jeff has him crated and ready to go."

"He's okay?" Louis asked.

"Good to go." Katy smiled. "He'll do better out there than in here." She pulled off her apron and looked at her watch. "We need to do it at dusk because they feel safer then. So, you want to come?"

"Wouldn't miss it for the world," Louis said.

The setting sun was just starting to singe the tops of the cypress trees when Jeff slowed the swamp buggy. Riding in the passenger seat, Louis had a clear view of the landscape but still no idea where they were. He suspected that unlike Katy, who seemed as at home in the Glades as the panthers, he would never feel like anything but an intruder in this primordial place.

He had come to appreciate its desolate beauty, come to understand its strange pull on the soul. But he still didn't belong here.

Jeff stopped the swamp buggy. The quiet, after the roar of the engine, was almost deafening. Katy, who had been riding in the back with another ranger, jumped out and came up to Louis.

"You sure you want to mess up those nice shoes?" she asked, smiling.

"Screw the shoes. Let's go."

It took all four of them to lift the crate down from the buggy. It was solid wood except for the breathing holes so Louis couldn't see Bruce. He could only hear him, hear his anxious panting.

Louis had sweated through his white dress shirt by the time they set the crate down on the marshy ground. He wiped his face, looking around.

They were somewhere deep in the preserve and Katy had chosen an isolated hammock for the release site, an island of brush and trees that sat a foot or so above the shallow water.

There was a low fringe of dark green on the far horizon and above that the sky was a huge blister of purple and orange. They had maybe ten minutes of daylight left.

"Let's do it," Katy said.

She went to the front of the crate and grasped the handle in the front. She gave it a hard tug upward.

"Go," she said softly.

The panther was a brown blur and it took Louis's eyes a second to catch up with Bruce. He was running across the open field at full speed. Then with a splash of his hind legs in the shallow water, he was gone.

Louis stared at the spot in the dark brush where the panther had disappeared.

"Where's he going?" he said.

"North," Katy said.

She stood staring into the darkness. "It's still mating season," she said. "He'll travel hundreds of miles to find a mate if he has to."

They stood silent for a moment then Katy let out a long breath, turned and walked back to the swamp buggy.

Louis didn't move. He looked east, where the rising moon was a pale sliver and Venus burned bright. He looked west, where a flock of egrets seeking a roosting place slid silently across the purple sky. He looked north, where the panther had gone.

And he knew.

He knew in that moment what he had to do. He still wanted the badge but it would have to wait a little while longer. He was okay with that now. Because it gave him a little time. Time to make things right with the two most important people in his life. Before he set foot in that academy Louis knew he had to go north, for just a while.

North, where Lily waited for a birthday party.

North, where maybe, just maybe, Joe still waited for him.

NEW RELEASE PREVIEW

THE DAMAGE DONE

CHAPTER ONE

S omething was wrong. This wasn't where he was supposed to be.

Louis Kincaid leaned forward and peered out the windshield. The gray stone building in front of him went in and out of focus with each sweep of the wipers, appearing and disappearing in the rain like a medieval castle on some lost Scottish moor.

But it was just an abandoned church, sitting in a weedy lot in a rundown neighborhood in Lansing, Michigan. Louis picked up the piece of paper on which he had scribbled the directions. It was the right address, but this couldn't be the place where he had come to start his life over again.

He rested his hands on the steering wheel and stared at the church. A car went by slowly and pulled up to the curb, parking in front of him, maybe fifteen feet away. Louis sat up, alert. It was a black Crown Vic with tinted windows and a small antenna mounted on the trunk. But it was plate that gave it away -- three letters and three numbers, just like all Michigan plates, but this one had an X in the middle.

An unmarked cop car. The driver didn't get out. But he didn't have to. Louis knew who it was.

The devil. It was the devil himself.

As Louis waited for the man to emerge, all the doubts that had chewed on him for the last three days, piling up during the thirteen-hundred-mile drive up from Florida, were now pushing to the front of his brain, coalescing into one big question.

Was this a mistake? He had a sure thing going back in Florida, a new start wearing a deputy's badge again. But this...this was the promise of something so much grander, to be on the ground floor of an elite new homicide task force. And to be back in Michigan near his daughter Lily and his lover Joe.

But at what price?

The door of the Crown Vic opened and the man got out. He pulled up the collar of his windbreaker and reached in the back for a small cardboard box. Louis sat forward to get a good look at his face. He hadn't seen the man since that day back in 1985 when he had vowed that Louis would never work as a cop again in Michigan.

Six years had gone by since. Six long years spent in exile.

But now Louis was back. And the same man who had taken his life away was now offering him a chance at a new one.

Mark Steele hurried up the walk and unlocked the church's front door. It wasn't until Steele disappeared inside that Louis sat back in the seat. For a long time he sat there, then he finally pulled the keys from the ignition.

There was no point in sitting here any longer. The bargain had been made. It was time to face him. Louis got out of the Mustang, jogged through the rain to the wooden doors of the church and slipped quietly inside.

The church was empty, emptied of almost everything that told of its true function. The pews were stacked like old cordwood in a corner. There was a shadow on the floor where the stone baptismal fountain once stood. The faint outline of a large crucifix was visible above the altar. A cold wind swirled around him but he couldn't tell where it was coming from. Then he looked up and saw a broken pane in the large stained glass window behind the altar.

But he didn't see Mark Steele.

Louis moved slowly through the nave, his eyes wandering up over the dark wood beams, the ornate pendant lamps, and finally down to the dark carved paneling scarred with graffiti.

What had happened to this place? How had it come to be left to ruin? Why had they given him the address of an old church instead of the task force's new headquarters? And what was Steele doing here?

Whooooooo...ahhhh.

His eyes shot upward. *What the hell?*

The sound came again, deep and mournful, floating on the cold air from somewhere on high.

He saw the source. Up in the choir balcony above the entrance. Just the wind moving through the old pipes of the organ.

Louis scanned the shadowed corners but there was no sign of Steele. Louis decided to wait and looked around for somewhere to sit, but the only thing he saw was an old low-slung slat-backed chair up on the altar. He mounted the four carpeted steps, unzipped his parka and sat down, rubbing his eyes. He had driven almost straight through from Fort Myers, the backseat of his Mustang packed with his suitcases, boxes and Issy wailing in a cat carrier. A driving April rain had found him in Ohio and had stayed with him all the way here to the state capital.

Louis leaned his head back and closed his eyes. The soft wail of the wind in the organ came and went, lulling him. He wasn't sure how long he stayed like that, but suddenly the air around him changed — the cold displaced with something warmer. He opened his eyes.

Mark Steele was standing at the foot of the altar.

"You're supposed to kneel," Steele said.

"Excuse me?" Louis said.

Steele nodded at the wooden chair Louis was sitting in. "That's not a chair, it's a *prie-dieu*. You're supposed to kneel on it, not sit."

Louis rose, his eyes locked on Steele.

The man hadn't changed in six years. Except for the clothes. The last time Louis had seen Steele, he had been all starched white shirt, black suit and clean iron jaw. Now he was wearing jeans, a blue state police windbreaker and a day's growth of whiskers.

It struck him again how odd it was that Steele had offered him this job without even one in-person interview. The first phone call had come out of the blue on a breezy Florida day a few months ago, from a woman with a velvety voice. She identified herself only as Camille Gaudaire, Mark Steele's personal aide, and said Steele was offering him the chance to be part of a five-man elite homicide squad working for the State of Michigan.

He had one day to decide.

Louis had spent the next few hours walking on the beach, trying to work past his shock, telling himself that this must be some kind of joke or worse, some kind of weird Karmic trap. His gut still churned with anger at Mark Steele but his heart ached for a chance to be closer to the woman he loved and the daughter he needed to know. And to wear the badge he so desperately missed. In the end, he knew this was his best chance to get back to Michigan, and by sundown, he had called Camille back to accept.

Louis came down the steps. There were a dozen things he wanted to ask Steele, hard questions about their volatile past and what appeared to be a chancy future, but instead he found himself extending his hand.

"Thank you for this opportunity," Louis said.

Steele held Louis's eyes for a second then shook his hand. "Don't thank me yet," he said. "This type of unit is new to the state. Things are still in flux. There's a chance this job may not turn out to be what you hope it is."

Louis stared at him.

"It may not turn out to be what *I* hope it is," Steele added. He moved away, his eyes wandering up over the beams and down to the scarred paneling. He turned back to Louis.

"What do you think?" he asked.

"About what, sir?"

"Our new home."

For a second, Louis thought it was a joke, but Steele's expression was deadpan. This was going to be the task force's permanent headquarters?

"It's...unusual," Louis said.

"You don't like churches?"

How to answer that one? His experience with churches was limited to snapshot memories of sitting on a hard bench in a hot clapboard building in Blackpool, Mississippi trying to catch the air from the women's fans. Or those cold Sundays sitting next to his foster mother Frances in the drafty Presbyterian Church in Plymouth, so very aware of being the only black face in a field of white.

Steele was looking up to the choir balcony. "Lansing has quite a few abandoned churches, so I got a good break on the rent," he said. He looked back to Louis. "I'd rather spend the money on other things."

"I thought we'd be working out of the state police headquarters," Louis said.

"When you work in a glass cubicle you get a glass cubicle mind. You get cautious. You get limited. You worry about impressing the wrong people. I don't want people like that working for me. We need to be independent."

Steele went to a bank of doors, opened one of the confessional booths and peered inside. "We'll set the desks up here in the nave. There's also a kitchen and bunkrooms in the basement," he said. "We'll need them."

Louis looked around, envisioning long hours and living on coffee and takeout. Camille Gaudaire hadn't told him much, only that he would be one of five members of a special squad assembled to work on unsolved homicides, cases that had been long ago abandoned by local police. Lots of travel and long hours. And, given the fact this squad was Steele's baby, probably a lot of pressure to not screw up.

Steele's voice broke into his thoughts. "I imagine you have a few more questions for me but put them on hold for now. I don't want to have to repeat myself five times so we'll clear things up at our first meeting."

Louis doubted that his particular questions could be cleared up at a staff meeting. They were too personal, still too raw, the experience in Loon Lake too vivid, even after six years.

"You find a place to live yet?" Steele asked.

Louis shook his head. "I just got in."

Steele nodded. "Check the *State Journal* classifieds. There are decent rentals near campus. We start back here Monday morning."

Two days? No way would this place be ready in two days. Again, the question was there. What the hell had he gotten himself into? He knew what cops were like, how they protected their turfs. What kind of politics and shit went into building an investigative unit that operated separate from the usual lines of authority and webs of bureaucracy?

And again, stuck inside him like a hard driven nail, the question: How in the hell could he trust this man? If something went wrong, if he screwed up just once, Louis had no doubt he'd be out, with no chance of ever wearing a badge again anywhere. There were no guarantees, no protection.

Steele headed toward the door. Louis followed slowly, feeling an urge to linger just a bit longer in his new home. When Steele pulled open the door, he paused and looked back at the empty nave, like a man surveying a newly purchased fixer-upper.

For some reason Louis felt compelled to fill the silence. "There's nothing here," he said.

"I have everything I need," Steele said. "I have the right people."

Steele pushed through the door and Louis followed him out. The rain had stopped but late afternoon fog was like being wrapped in gray felt. Louis watched as Steele locked the door, then went down the steps, over to the squat stone pillar on the lawn and removed the FOR LEASE sign. He went to the Crown Vic, popped the trunk and tossed in the sign. He turned back to Louis, still standing on the steps.

"Monday morning," Steele said. "Nine o'clock."

Then he was gone.

Louis zipped up his parka and looked back at the church. The stone pillar where the FOR LEASE sign had been now was bare except for the Bible verse on it. Some of the letters were missing but Louis could still read it.

The new creation has come.

The old has gone, the new is here! – 2 Corinthians

Louis's eyes went to the name of the church on the top of the sign. It hadn't registered the first time he saw it but it did now. SAINT MICHAEL'S CATHOLIC CHURCH.

Michael...the patron saint of cops.

CHAPTER TWO

When Louis walked into St. Michaels on Monday morning he didn't recognize the place. The old stone floor had the gleaming look of a pressure-cleaned patio and the graffiti had been scoured off the confessionals. The stack of pews had been re-moved and the flaking walls had been re-plastered.

The sides of the nave had been outfitted with five plain metal desks, each topped with a computer monitor. There was a long table in the middle of the nave, a gleaming mahogany monstrosity that looked like it had come from a corporate boardroom. Four black telephones were clustered in the middle of the table.

Louis glanced at his watch. Twenty to nine. Apparently, he was the first one to arrive. His decision to get here early wasn't an attempt to suck up to Steele. It was more because Louis had barely slept since his arrival Friday, his usual insomnia made worse by the *rumble-blat* of I-96 outside his Super 8 room, and the rattle of the ice machine in the hall.

Two days of searching and he hadn't been able to find an apartment. Stupid to think he would, given that spring semester was just starting up again at Michigan State. He just prayed he could find a place tonight before some maid discovered Issy cowering under the bed.

He looked at his watch again. Where were the other squad members? He was anxious to meet them to assess who he was working with.

He moved toward the altar. The beautiful stonework and murals were now hidden by three bulletin boards and a large green chalkboard, the kind that could be wheeled around and flipped. He felt a stream of cold air and looked up. The stained-glass window was still missing its pane.

As he took a step back to get a better look at the window Louis saw that it depicted Jesus surrounded by a cluster of men in robes and beards. The apostles, he guessed. The cold breeze was coming from the man kneeling at Jesus's feet –– it was the missing pane. The guy had no face.

A door banged shut and Louis turned to the front door, expecting Steele or one of the other unit members. But it was a workman carrying a power tool. Two other workers drifted in, carrying boxes emblazoned with the word DELL. They gave Louis a quick glance before splitting off and disappearing beneath the desks.

Louis moved to a desk to look at one of the computers. They were alien to him. He realized that being out of law enforcement for so long, he was already miles behind whatever technology the state of Michigan was probably using. Hell, he wasn't even sure he could figure out how to run his own wants and warrants checks. His best friend back in Florida, Mel Landeta, had something called a MacIntosh, and Louis had meant to ask for a tutorial. But after that first phone call from Steele's aide, Camille Gaudaire, there had been no time.

Camille had told him that there would be some follow-up interviews and paperwork, then she gave him some concise marching orders: He had to get in top physical shape. He had to qualify on handgun, long rifle, assault rifle and shotgun. He had to familiarize himself with Michigan's most infamous unsolved homicides. Then Camille laid out the kicker.

You must attain a rudimentary knowledge of a foreign language. The captain knows you took French in college. He expects you to become fluent as quickly as possible.

Louis didn't ask why. He just got to work. For the next three months, he worked his ass off. Pumped iron in Fort Myers gyms until he couldn't make a fist. Tried to memorize the Michigan State Police policy and procedures manual. Faxed Camille the results of his physical and his firing range scores. Took a French adult ed course and fell asleep each night to the sing-song sound of a strange woman conjugating verbs. He also read every book and article he could find on Michigan homicides, never sure he had the right ones, or if he was learning from them what Steele expected him to learn. And he turned down the offer he had with the Lee County Sheriff's office, giving up a sure thing for this flyer of a job, so he could be just hours away from Lily and Joe.

Ils aiment. Nous aimons. Vous aimes. J'aimes

They love. We love. You love

I love...

A sharp whirring noise made Louis start. The guy with the power tool was crouched atop the conference table and was drilling holes in the center. When he paused to adjust his safety glasses, he saw Louis and gave him a twisted smile.

"Never had to run phone lines in a church before," he said. He made the sign of the cross over his sweatshirt and went back to his drilling.

From somewhere deep in the bowels of the church came the sound of hammering. Every time it stopped, Louis could hear the wheeze of the wind through the pipe organ up in the choir loft.

The banging of the front door closing made Louis turn.

The man standing at the entrance was big, at least six-foot-seven, with a bald bullet head sticking out of a worn black leather bomber jacket and meaty bowed legs encased in faded black jeans. As he came forward, the man took off his mirrored sunglasses, revealing two white raccoon patches pinpricked with small bloodshot blue eyes.

The guy had to be a member of the unit, but he looked like he had just gotten off a three-day bender at Daytona Bike Week.

He came forward and gave Louis a once over, and for a second Louis saw himself in the man's eyes –- new blue blazer, slacks, tie, and white shirt so fresh from the dry cleaners it still had creases down the front.

The guy took an unlit cigarillo stub from his mouth and smiled, revealing big movie-star teeth. "You with the task force?" he asked.

"Yeah," Louis answered. He stuck out his hand. "Louis Kincaid."

"Cam Bragin."

The guy had a vice-grip. When he let go, Louis resisted the urge to shake the blood back into his hand. But he did take a step back, to distance himself from the burnt cherry smell of the cigarillo.

The front doors banged open again. A large woman with wild gray hair, carrying a briefcase and wearing a bright red cape, paused just inside, her eyes wandering up over the beams and windows. With a flourish, she flung off her cape.

A man appeared behind her, as if by the magic of her cape's movement –- short, wiry, dark floppy hair and black-rimmed glasses. He wore baggy khakis and a green windbreaker. There was a huge mail pouch slung over his concave chest.

Before either of them could say hello, Louis heard the echo of footsteps somewhere up high and looked up to the choir loft.

Mark Steele was leaning on the railing gazing down at them. Then he disappeared from view and reappeared on the spiral staircase curling down to the nave. Steele was dressed all in black -- open collar black shirt, trousers. All eyes were on Steele as he came up to the conference table. Even the guy running the phone lines had stopped his drilling to stare.

"Can you work somewhere else for a while?" Steele asked the man.

"It's your dime, I'm on triple overtime, and need a smoke," the phone man said as he headed toward the door. As if by heavenly decree, all other banging and clanging in the church stopped.

Steele was holding a small cardboard box, the same one he had brought in the first time Louis had seen him. He set it down on the conference table. "Please, all of you take a seat," he said.

Louis took the chair closest to Steele. Cam sat down next to him and the two others grabbed chairs on the far side. The woman had a difficult time arranging her cape and briefcase in her chair and Steele waited, but not without a glimmer of annoyance.

"We have two people who have not arrived," Steele began. "Our fifth team member will be coming to us from the FBI, area of expertise psychology and profiling."

A sharp clang made Steele stop. His eyes shot to a worker who was picking a wrench off the stone floor. Steele waited until the man had disappeared before he went on.

"The second person you have all talked to by phone," Steele said. "She is Camille Gaudaire, my sénéchal." He surveyed the blank faces before he looked at Louis. "Translation?"

He didn't know the word sénéchal, so he decided to guess. "Assistant?"

"Close but not quite right. She is my consigliere and will be your coordinator and chief contact."

Steele turned to his left. "First, let me introduce you to each other. This is Cameron Bragin. After serving his country, Cam went into police work in Chicago, distinguishing himself in undercover work. He's been ass-deep in narcotics, gun trafficking, prostitution, organized crime, everything on the criminal menu, but has never once been made. So, if you need undercover infiltration, male or female, he's your man. Or woman, if you will."

Louis couldn't help but think that any perp who took Cam Bragin for a woman had to be blind.

Steele said something to Cam in what sounded like Russian or Polish. Cam replied with a chuckle.

"Next up is Junia Cruz," Steele said, turning to the other side of the table. "Junia's from the City of Angels, where she has discovered there are few. She's an expert in cutting edge crime scene investigations, forensics, blood spatter, bullet trajectory. She has significant contacts in the most advanced labs and universities in the country, so use her."

Steele paused for a second, as if trying to remember something, then spoke to Junia in Spanish. "*Los muertos siempre dicen la verdad, no?*"

"Si," Junia said with a smile.

Steele gave a nod to the small, dark-haired man. "Sanjay Thukkiandi. He likes to be called Tooki. He brings with him six years as an investigator in Madras, India, and three years as the FBI's leading computer tech expert. But maybe the best way to introduce Tooki is to quote something he told Camille during his interview. 'Like my computers, I am a complex machine, built of spare parts from the Madras gutters, the bowels of the FBI and the trash cans of Microsoft.'"

Tooki's cheeks reddened and he lowered his head.

Steele went on. "Tooki is not only an investigator in his own right, he is our technology expert. If the information you need is on a database somewhere in this country, he can find it for you. He'll also be working on linking us up to NCIC, VICAP, the new AFIS network, and as they go live, other databases that will allow us to search shoe and tire tread prints. I would welcome Tooki in what I have been told is Tamil, but that is one language I am still learning."

"Don't bother, Captain," Tooki said. "We've so bastardized it where I come from, I'm not sure I would understand proper Tamil anymore. Plain English is fine with me."

Steele gave him a smile. Louis suspected Steele would try to learn the language anyway, just to prove he could.

Steele's eyes moved to Louis. "Louis Kincaid," he said. "Criminology degree from University of Michigan, ex-patrolman, ex-detective, lionized in multiple law publications as Florida's premier private eye and the captor of Florida's Paint it Black serial killer."

Louis wondered if the edge he heard in Steele's voice was ridicule or respect for the tabloid notoriety Louis had gained.

"Louis has been studying to become our in-house expert on unsolved Michigan homicides," Steele said. He paused with the barest of smiles and added, "Louis has exceptional instincts and a special feel for unsolved cases that you will all come to appreciate."

Louis held Steele's hard brown eyes, not happy with the description of his resume. It made his past sound sensational and his investigative skills almost paranormal. That's the last thing he needed with this group -- to be tagged as some sort of celebrity mystic who dug through dusty folders.

"Louis," Steele said, *"bon retour chez toi."*

Welcome home? Louis was so surprised it took him a moment to answer. "It's good to be back," he said.

"Now, as I told all of you, this task force will be focusing on Michigan's unsolved homicide cases," Steele said. "I have loosely modeled it after one of the first squads of this type, a three-man team formed in Miami eight years ago to solve the old murder of a young girl. A local reporter dubbed them the Cold Case Squad and the name stuck."

Louis had a vague memory of hearing about this squad at one point. His lover Joe had worked for Miami PD – had she mentioned it?

"As you may have guessed, I have a special affection for unsolved cases," Steele said. "I fought hard not only to establish this unit but to get the funding and equipment we will need to be successful."

Steele's eyes moved around the faces at the table, holding the moment on edge as skillfully as anyone Louis had ever met. Even the wind was still.

"I am a believer in the power of justice," Steele continued. "Not because it brings closure to the families, because it can't. And not because it allows us, as a society, to get revenge by incarcerating the offender for the rest of his life because, as we all know, for many prison is not the hell we wish it was."

Steele took a deep breath.

"I believe in justice because it restores a balance," he said. "Not only in the broad philosophical sense of the way our world is supposed to work, but more importantly, in each of you. And you, above all others, need that balance. Do you all understand?"

Someone murmured a yes. Louis looked down at his leather folder, his thoughts drawn back to a PI case he worked in Florida, where the need to catch a killer had a compelled him to not only beat the shit out of the man, but to bury a piece of evidence in order to send him off to jail.

"To paraphrase Malcom X," Steele said. "Our mission first is truth, no matter what it is, and then justice, no matter who it is for or against."

Louis was still back in Florida, remembering. Although he hadn't recognized it at the time, he had sought this balance Steele talked about because he had thought seeing the killer in jail would bring him that. But it had brought him nothing because in what he had done, there had been no truth. In the end, he had returned the evidence anonymously to the local PD.

"Now that we have all that out of the way, let's get down to basics," Steele said. "You will all be issued a new Michigan-blue Ford Explorer, equipped with video cameras, shotguns, rifles and a long-range state of the art radio that will allow you to communicate with the sénéchal from almost anywhere in the lower peninsula. The radio will also come with pre-set frequencies that will allow you to communicate with most major agencies in the state."

"Sweet," Cam said softly.

"In order to travel as cases dictate, you will all have a go-bag with you at all times," Steele went on. "You will also each receive a pager and a cellular telephone. These phones are high-tech experimental models designed to work with radio frequencies and should give you service anywhere your radio works. But they are not a hundred percent reliable so please keep that in mind when you are working in a desolate area."

Louis saw Tooki nodding.

"They're also expensive to operate," Steele said. "Excessive charges will be taken out of your paycheck. And don't lose them. That cost, too, will be deducted from your check."

Louis lowered his head to hide his smile. For the first time in years, he was going to have a regular paycheck and it was going to be big. If he decided to impress his daughter Lily by calling her on the damn phone at least now he could afford it.

"In general, your schedule will be dictated by your work load," Steele said. "Even though you are all salaried, you will log your hours and travel expenses with the sénéchal. I expect a six-day work week, no less than ten hours a day. We are converting the basement here to bunk rooms and there is a full kitchen, so when the work dictates that I need you here together, at least you will be comfortable."

Steele reached into his box and retrieved a thick blue binder Louis recognized as the procedure manual.

"You've all read this by now, I'm sure," Steele said. "Make sure you know the rules but keep in mind, in the end, at any given moment, you will be the one who makes those instant decisions we all face from time to time. Exigent circumstances, use of force, how far and how hard to push a suspect."

The room was quiet, except for the whistle of the wind through the broken pane in the stained glass window.

"Be aggressive but be smart," Steele said, "because the first time your reckless decision costs us an innocent life, gets a case thrown out of court or brings unnecessary shit raining down, you're finished. Not just with me, but in the entire state. Are we clear?"

Louis looked away. In other words, exile.

When no one said anything, Steele went on. "One more thing before you get your first assignments."

Steele opened the cardboard box and withdrew a handful of black leather wallets. "Your credentials," he said.

One by one, he checked the name on the inside then slid the wallet across the table to its owner.

Louis opened his wallet. On one side was his ID card, the photo taken a few weeks ago on one of his trips up from Florida for new-hire processing. His eyes moved down the type. Louis W. Kincaid, Detective, State of Michigan.

On the other side of the fold was a gold shield cushioned in black leather. An embossed eagle sat atop the MSP emblem of two elk on their hind legs, bookending a man holding a flag. Under that were the words: *si quaeris peninsulam amoenam circumspice.*

He could still remember the translation of the state motto from his police academy days: *If you seek a beautiful peninsula, look about you.*

There was a lone word in the middle of the badge -- *TUEBOR. I will defend.*

"When you're all done admiring your gold, I'll ask you all to stand up and raise your right hand."

The sound of chairs scraping across the stone floor filled the nave.

Steele opened a small black notebook. "Repeat after me. I...do solemnly swear..."

Louis' face grew warm as the murmur of voices echoed softly through the church. For a split-second, it almost seemed a dream but he knew it wasn't. He was back. He was finally back.

"That I will faithfully discharge the duties of an officer of the Michigan State police..."

Louis looked around the table. Everyone had the same expression -- restrained excitement and pride.

"With the authority invested in me," Steele said, "I appoint you detectives of the department of Michigan state police. Congratulations."

Louis sat down, his eyes moving back to his open badge. Then he closed the wallet and looked back at Steele.

"Our first couple cases will come directly from the state's attorney general and his office is currently reviewing requests from local agencies," Steele said. "So, to keep you busy, I have selected unsolved cases for you to work on. Consider these cases a getting-your-feet-wet process. You're not being tested but you will be studied. What I want is to see is how your mind works, how you utilize your tools, your skills and those of your partners. This process will help solidify you as a team."

Steele went up to the altar, dragged the large green chalk board to the center and flipped the board over. On the other side were five large photographs. Above each was a case number and a brief description written in chalk.

The Dumpster Hookers 1988.
CMU Death Ring. Suicides/homicides? 1990.
Palmer Park Wolf Pack murders 1985.
The Bay City Black Widow. 1989.
Boys in the Box. Copper Harbor. Found 1979. Died?

Junia was the first to get up and go up to the altar for a closer look. Cam and Tooki followed. Louis joined them, standing at the bottom of the stairs, eyeing the photos.

They were grainy blow-ups, obviously taken from case files. The bloodied nude body of a woman lying next to a garbage bin. A young man hanging in a shower stall. A battered body sprawled in a field of wild flowers. A whale-like bloated body on a rocky beach.

When Louis got to the last photograph, he took a step closer.

It was a color picture but faded to orange, as photographs from the seventies often were. It showed two small skulls lying on their right sides inches apart on a wooden surface.

"Louis."

It took him a moment to realize Steele was talking to him.

"Your pick."

"Excuse me, sir?"

"Cam has chosen the hookers, Junia the black widow. Your turn."

Louis glanced at Steele then looked back at the photograph of the skulls. It was the oldest case and he suspected it would be the toughest. He also knew he had to take it.

"The boys in the box," he said.

MEET PJ PARRISH

www.pjparrish.com

P.J. Parrish is *the New York Times* bestselling author of ten Louis Kincaid and Joe Frye thrillers. The author is actually two sisters, Kristy Montee and Kelly Nichols. Their books have appeared on both the New York Times and USA Today best seller lists. The series has garnered 11 major crime-fiction awards, and an Edgar® nomination. Parrish has won two Shamus awards, one Anthony and one International Thriller award. Her books have been published throughout Europe and Asia.

Parrish's short stories have also appeared in many anthologies, including two published by Mystery Writers of America, edited by Harlan Coben and the late Stuart Kaminsky. Their stories have also appeared in Akashic Books acclaimed DETROIT NOIR, and in Ellery Queen Magazine. Most recently, they contributed an essay to a special edition of Edgar Allan Poe's works edited by Michael Connelly.

Before turning to writing full time, Kristy Montee was a newspaper editor and dance critic for the Sun-Sentinel in Fort Lauderdale. Nichols previously was a blackjack dealer and then a human resources specialist in the casino industry. Kristy lives in Tallahassee Fla., and Traverse City, Mich. Kelly resides in Traverse City. The sisters were writers as kids, albeit with different styles: Kelly's first attempt at fiction at age 11 was titled "The Kill." Kristy's at 13 was "The Cat Who Understood." Not much has changed: Kelly now tends to handle the gory stuff and Kristy the character development. But the collaboration is a smooth one, thanks to lots of ego suppression, good wine, and marathon phone calls via Skype.

BOOKS BY PJ PARRISH

DARK OF THE MOON
DEAD OF WINTER
PAINT IT BLACK
THICKER THAN WATER
ISLAND OF BONES
A KILLING RAIN
THE UNQUIET GRAVE
A THOUSAND BONES
SOUTH OF HELL
THE LITTLE DEATH
THE KILLING SONG
CLAW BACK
(A Louis Kincaid Novella)
HEART OF ICE
SHE'S NOT THERE
THE DAMAGE DONE